THE GIRL WITH THE IMAGINATION OF WIZARDS

By Gary Miles

Copyright © 2024 Gary Miles

All rights reserved. No part of this text may be reproduced, stored in a retrieval system, or transmitted, in any form or by any means, whether electrical, mechanical, photocopying, recording, or otherwise, without the prior permission of the author.

Cover illustration by Amanda Gazidis

Contents

THIS DREAM OF LIGHT

1. THE BOY WHO WASN'T REAL 1
2. MIDSUMMER QUEEN 7
3. A CONVERSATION WITH PUCK 10
4. AN AWED ENCOUNTER IN A DREAM 13
5. THE WISDOM HEAD 24
6. SHEELA TELLS HER STORY 32
7. SHEELA FINISHES HER STORY 49
8. THE SONGS OF SPRING 55
9. AN UNSEELIE CELEBRATION 59

EPILOGUE 68

THE CASE STUDY OF CHILD A 74

FLOWERS AND FAES 76

GIRL WITH IMAGINATION OF WIZARDS 77

GLOSSARY 78

THE LEGEND OF THE CHANGELING 80

THIS DREAM OF LIGHT

Where is the place where dreams are kept?
Is it the Garden with Many Names?
Dream of a place with late sunsets
Even night is bright in this domain

It's hard to tell when the Sun starts rising
Much easier to wake up worshipping
Later you sit with flowers, slow your breathing
When you sleep, you dream you are the flower's king

This dream of light is the Sun's (by right)
Offer it to his rays
If he is pleased, he will choose this dream
to light the Longest Day

The fullest day dawns today
The Sun has favoured you
If you are pleased, bless his beams
Praise all the bright nights too

1. THE BOY WHO WASN'T REAL

Bobby had gone up to the counter and was ordering jam doughnuts for us. It had been an eventful morning and we needed something sweet.

"You got me worried back there, Jimi. There's a time to swim and it's not when the tide's pulling you away. You're lucky you weren't swept out to sea."

"Stop exaggerating, Avie Smith. I know you care but there's nothing worse than a schoolgirl know-it-all."

"You were the one calling for help."

The air was close in the café even by the entrance where we were sitting. Music was blaring from the rides on the pier. Hits about spacemen played at a far louder volume than a transistor radio could ever manage. The rides were busy judging by the queues of teenagers we could make out through the window above our table.

Bobby returned with a tray full of the most delicious West Country doughnuts. "There's a hot chocolate for you Jimi. Drink it and you'll be better in no time."

"Thanks, Bobby," I said taking a big bite out of my doughnut.

"And thank you for getting me back to the beach," added Jimi.

"It was lucky for you I hadn't finished my dip. And that I saw you struggling." Bobby mimed a boy drowning. It was so funny. Even Jimi laughed.

Bobby had stopped being a stranger even before we'd entered the café but by the time we were walking home, he had become our friend. I was already friends with Jimi, we were in the same class together, but it felt good to have someone new join us.

The hour-long walk from the seaside to our village was ideal for talking while the country lanes Bobby took us through were so quiet we barely noticed any traffic. He struck us as being older than we were but it wasn't easy working out his age. He was currently living with a farmer and his family. The farmer had a spare room in his farmhouse, he let Bobby stay there, even paying him a small wage, in return for help on the land.

Bobby had lived somewhere else before coming to the village; we were intrigued to know where. But no matter how many questions we asked him he remained silent about his past. Our curiosity grew in the weeks that followed but not until we broke up for the half-term holiday would we get any answers.

One Thursday, at the end of May, found the three of us walking toward the pier. The farmer had just paid Bobby his wages and he wanted to treat us by taking us on some rides.

Now, this Thursday was a market day, and knowing we were always hungry after the rides, Bobby suggested we should stop off at the market first and buy food there. They sold the most mouth-watering cakes and fruits at the stalls and the cheap tasty food would leave us more money for the rides.

"I expect we'll see the girl there," Jimi sighed.

"You're not speaking about your girlfriend?" teased Bobby. "You don't look older than ten or eleven."

"He's the same age as me, Bobby."

"Just about, I'll be twelve in the summer hols, Avie."

Jimi can usually take teasing so there must be something we didn't know to explain the change that came over him as he continued: more seriously.

"Wait until you see her. She goes to the market to get help. She's always there on market day."

Bobby went quiet for a moment and his face paled.

The girl was there just beyond the last stall, we saw her propped up, in a corner, against a wall. All her possessions – her whole world – filled a battered carrier bag. The blanket spread over her knees looked as thin as her clothes. Within minutes of seeing her, we found out what she needed and by the time we left the market, we'd fulfilled her requests.

There was no sense going to the pier now. We had spent so much money helping the girl we hadn't enough left for the rides! It was a pity, as I had been looking forward to the dodgems while the boys had been eager to try their luck at the riffle range. It was too early to go home yet. So we agreed, we'd continue onto the seafront anyhow. Once there we would decide what to do.

It was later on that Thursday that Bobby dropped a little of his secrecy and let us know some more about him.

"My mother had this strange belief about me. She thought I was a changeling! My father encouraged this belief, it was his desire she wouldn't love me."

Jimi was puzzled. "A changeling?"

Unlike Jimi, I knew what a changeling was. My mum has told me stories about the supernatural and I couldn't believe anyone could suspect our friend Bobby of not being human.

"If I remember rightly ... it's a child that looks human but in reality it was left by fairies!"

"You remember the legends right, Avie. My parents made me feel different from them. And from anyone else! Maybe it was true!"

Bobby's story (told over a walk) seemed a good way of passing the time. But neither Jimi nor I had expected his story to begin so bleakly.

Now, the promenade we were walking along looked out at two contrasting scenes. On one side, you passed grass and flowerbeds and on the other side, you could access the beach. There was a bandstand in the middle of the grass; opposite it was an empty seat. A few feet from the bench there stood a coin-operated telescope pointing out to sea.

Bobby seemed to be looking through his own mental telescope as he described his past with his parents to us. All magnified and brought near, its pain better seen.

"As I wasn't their 'real child' it didn't matter to them that I was lonely, or that they frightened me. I began wasting away with no strength to be constantly working. Running away was an act of self-preservation!"

Bobby's eyes began to tear up but he didn't cry. I admired his effort to talk calmly about his experiences as a 'street kid'. Bobby couldn't recall how long he'd been out on the streets. But he remembered with gratitude an old man who found him lying in a doorway and offered him shelter.

"So that winter didn't claim me as her victim."

"That was kind of him, taking you in. But who was he?" asked Jimi.

"I didn't know at first ... I'm still not sure now. But he wanted me to be strong again for the spring."

"We'd like to thank him. Wouldn't we, Jimi."

"He didn't do what he did for praise, Avie. He was truly a kind man. And the more time I spent with him the more I came to trust him.

"Having won my trust, he let me in on a secret. He showed me this picture of this huge, beautiful garden. He said he was my father. My real father! And if I tried hard enough I would remember him. I'd remember the garden.

"I wasn't sure what to make of this revelation. If I'd ever lived in a garden paradise, I'd remember it, surely. And I'm even less sure how I feel about those missing years before I was a changeling. If that's what I am. In the end, I decided to accept his story. I told him I remembered being his son."

Jimi's puzzlement was getting worse. "You're making yourself sound so mysterious, Bobby. I bet you were a normal baby. That means you can't have lived somewhere before."

"The truth is. I don't know. I want to prove him right. One day, I will. But for now my earliest days are a blank – a void!"

This sounded so tragic. I let out a shriek! Everyone started laughing at me. It felt good to release the tension.

Bobby ended his story by showing us something special.

"I do have something he gave me. Whenever I play it I feel him nearby."

"I bet it's a recorder."

"No, Avie. Now guess again."

"Then it's a flute?"

"You're getting warmer, Jimi... it's a piccolo!"

"Can you play it?" I asked. I'd never heard of a piccolo before.

Bobby rose up from the seat and crossed over to the bandstand. We followed and when others began to join us and formed a little crowd, we hoped this wouldn't spoil his performance.

Smiling, breathing through the mouthpiece, Bobby's fingers worked their magic and I could almost see the notes in the melody he played. Even the gulls seemed moved: as they soared and dived in the sky, happy to have inspired him. The notes flew with the gulls. The gulls flew with the notes.

After the crowd had clapped their applause and dispersed, I noticed how happy Bobby looked, full of pride with his demons seemingly exorcised.

We didn't have to walk back to the village, this time, but managed to get a bus back instead. The bus that picked us up only runs on Market Day. The driver of the bus was very understanding. He approved of us helping the homeless girl and let us off the full fare.

I learnt a little more about 'this garden' (which had piqued my interest from the start). Bobby confirmed that it was not a physical picture he had been shown.

"Nothing so crude as a photograph, either."

"So how did he show it to you?"

"We were relaxing, like meditating, with our eyes closed. And he put me into this 'twilight conscious state,' or so he called it. He described a place that was like paradise ... but real. And the words and the music made it visible to me."

I felt a thrill when he said "music"; I knew he'd been listening to the piccolo.

Bobby went silent after that. It would have been rude to question him further. The ride was soon over and I looked forward to hearing more from Bobby.

Sunday afternoons, in our village, usually involve a walk after the Sunday roast. And the place we go most frequently is a local hill (with some interesting history).

Come Midsummer's Eve, our parents were busy, and it seemed we'd have to abandon our evening on the hill. Thankfully, Bobby offered to take over the parental role.

"There's more to the hill than you suppose," Bobby confided once we were alone. "And there's no better place to be on Midsummer's Eve."

Once on top of the hill you look down upon the village and see the landscape stretching for miles around. A landscape filled with bigger, blue-tinted hills, rising and receding against the sky.

Midsummer's Eve was the best time. We could stay out late and have the time of our lives. But after walking up and down slopes and running through the wooded bits (my favourite), we sat down to rest and eat our tea.

The piccolo comes alive in outdoor settings. It was the second time Bobby had played for us. And it sounded even sweeter than when we'd heard him with all the gulls flying. We were tired after the day's activities but Bobby's music made our tiredness go away.

The notes were so lively. I heard trills, cheeps, chirps, and chuckling. I thought of birds and wanted to dance. Suddenly, without warning, Bobby let go of the piccolo and it carried on playing in mid-air. A beautiful bird chorus burst out above the hill.My heart leaped up! The piccolo played on in the midsummer sky. I fell asleep.

2. MIDSUMMER QUEEN

I woke to birdsong, sunlight and a sense of having been somewhere else.

It was morning. The sun had got up before me. My clothes were soaked with dew. I was about to ask my friends where we were when I realised I was alone. Rising, I called them. No one answered. I sat down again to think.

I remembered a piccolo, music that made me want to dance and sing, falling asleep, and then a dream. The dream was so out of the ordinary. The biggest dream I had ever had. It had cosmic significance.

But I struggled to get a clear view of it – all at once.

Dream pictures stayed out of focus. Dream voices were a strain to hear.

What is the point of remembering if I can't understand?

It occurred to me that if I started walking my dream might stop teasing me and become more helpful; then we would both have clarity. So I yawned, stretched, and started walking.

Those who have been on the hill will know that one of the paths you climb up takes you past a wall of rock. Even though this wall isn't high, you wouldn't want to climb it, because the tangle of weeds, bushes, and long grass growing at its base would make it almost impossible. Standing just clear of this undergrowth was a figure dressed in gauze. When I recognised her I was so surprised, I could have climbed that wall.

"What are you staring for? I'm not a real Queen. It's only fancy dress!"

"Of course it's fancy dress! What do you take me for? But it's astonishing all the same."

"There, I'll put my crown on. That should put you at ease."

"That's a splendid crown. I'd love to wear one like that."

"Maybe I'll let you, when I've finished with it! But first, I'd like to know what you're doing here. Are you on the way to the hotel? Our little 'Fairy Ball' didn't disturb the village, did it? You haven't been sent here to complain?"

I assured her I hadn't. And if there had been any disturbance, I'd slept right through it.

"Good. I don't like complainers. My name's Maeve, by the way. Don't be put off by these clothes," laughed Maeve. "I had so much fun last night; you can't blame a girl for not wanting it to end."

Introductions over, I asked if I could touch Maeve's crown and gown. What looked elegant at first glance turned out to be cheap and badly made. Even so, the style of clothing was ageless (like something you would expect in a fairy tale).

Maeve's boots didn't go with the rest of her outfit. The shoes she'd been dancing in were back at the hotel. She'd chosen these boots to take her morning walk in; despite the hotel being the first building you come to once you leave the hill.

Maeve informed me that she'd come down to the countryside, this weekend, for a conference.

"That's not nearly as dull as it sounds especially when it's about the Mind (although not as much fun as being at a party)."

While I was enjoying Maeve's company, my dream still wasn't making sense to me. The walk hadn't helped so far.

"I must go! It's been lovely meeting you. But I must go!"

Maeve stopped me going, "But, wait, you still haven't told me what you are doing here by yourself?" Then putting on a mock-stern voice Maeve pretended to give away who she really was. "Come answer, child. The Queen of the Fairies commands it!"

I could have danced for joy. I knew the truth, at last!

"Thank you! Oh, thank you! Thank you, Maeve."

"So I didn't frighten you then?"

"No! I know you're not the Queen of the Fairies. But I saw her. The real one! I did!"

Now, this hill was once the site of an Iron Age fort. The Celts had dwelt here. And there was a suspicion of a Druidic Connection.

But what of the older inhabitants of this hill – had it opened yesterday, had they come out of it to dance?

I started looking around me for marks on the grass.

"Oh, where's the ring? Their boots must have left a ring?"

"I can't see a ring ... oh but look! There it is!"

"Well spotted, Maeve. We're in the centre of their circle."

But that's your footsteps I'm looking at. You must have been going round in circles."

"But my feet didn't leave those prints? This matches up with my dream!"

"Does it? How exciting! There's a lot of truth in dreams. If you share it with me, I'll try to enlighten you."

I did share it. But not then – something happened then that almost made me doubt I was awake. My feet must have wanted to dance ... just like the fairies... because they were making movements without my noticing them. Having danced me to the undergrowth, my foot kicked out and something hard fell against my shoe.

I bent down to remove it.

"I see the Fairies have left you a gift."

Maeve's words were apt. For what seemed a stick was no such thing. I had discovered what I hadn't known was lost and by chance had found Bobby's piccolo. I thought back to last evening, had it really been up there in the sky?

3. A CONVERSATION WITH PUCK

My friends and I were not the only visitors to the hill on the night of my dream. At the bottom of the hill, there is a small field that has the most accessible path to the hilltop. There was only one car in the car park by the field that evening. And the owner of that car was dancing in the field to the music of a portable radio. The radio was a novelty being bigger and noisier than other radios in the West and having come from afar. He had just driven from a pub where the clientele had been too old for him so he'd had to make his own fun on his own. What better way to have fun than to test the advanced new radio set that he'd been lucky enough to buy from a market in Bristol. It was lucky for him that we hadn't seen him dancing as he was about to be made to look very silly.

It was an extra warm evening and the man had very little on except some beads around his neck, and a pair of y-fronts. His denim jacket and jeans, along with t-shirt, socks, and shoes, lay discarded on the grass by the radio.

I had seen headbanging, or 'freaking out' (as we called it back in the Seventies) on TV, and wondered it didn't make those who did it go dizzy. The man was saved from going dizzy by a high-pitched voice, which interrupted the rock music to poke fun at him.

"*That's a great way to celebrate Midsummer. But where are your wizard robes? Your hair and beard are not all that long. You must be a most junior magician!*"

The man stopped headbanging and began looking around for the voice. Had someone turned off his radio? And how comes he couldn't see anyone about? How dare they suggest his hair length and facial hair made him look like some crazy wizard!

The voice laughed finding the whole thing hilarious. The laughter was eerie and merry at the same time.

The man walked over to the radio. Was there something up with its tuning? Had it picked up a prankster channel? Why couldn't he have his rock tunes back? He was just about to pick it up off the grass when the eerie high-pitched voice cried, *"Dance!"* and the man's clothes got up off the ground and started leaping and jigging.

"Go join in the fun!" the voice instructed mischievously and it all ended with the man-giving chase to his clothes: as jeans, jacket, socks, shoes, and t-shirt went dancing up the path in a merry procession right up to the hilltop. If he had stopped chasing to look behind him, he would have seen a wee little man climb out of the radio and increase in size until it was four feet high.

This was Puck! Now, Puck never means any serious harm with his mischief and so with untroubled conscience, he looked up at a cloud and whistled. The top of the cloud moved in a tossing motion and Puck recognised the mane of his horse Nebula. Raindrops fell from the long flowing mane as the whole horse kicked and shook herself free from the cloud. A snowy horse shape descended to the ground.

Nebula greeted Puck with a snort. "Up to your tricks again? I should have sent the rain earlier to stop you acting the knave."

"It's good to be a knave sometimes," laughed Puck. Hoping that now his voice was lower (and his body larger), the horse would be less inclined to find fault. But Nebula still looked sternly at Puck, making Puck wonder about the horse's sense of humour.

"Maybe I'll leave his radio tuned into fairyland, so that when he comes back for it he'll have something cool to listen to," suggested Puck.

"It's the least you could do. And put a charm on the radio. One that will do him a good turn."

Puck left his luckiest charm on the radio and was about to climb onto the horse's back, "But, wait, we can't leave this hill yet. There's a sleeper here that I think we should meet."

"We're be late, Puck!" urged Nebula. Climb on."

"What are you afraid of? That when we see this girl we'll like her and take her with us?"

• • •

They did like me, and decided to take me with them, and this is how it happened.

Quickly assuming a chubby, elfin shape, Puck was ready to wake me. He didn't want me completely awake but I needed to be in a light enough sleep to hear him. A lot of what he said has since slipped my memory, but the gist of it was that he was a famous trickster: "A fairy, no less!" Despite having a reputation for mischief that had made it into countless pamphlets and plays, I had nothing to fear from him. He was my friend and wanted to take me with him to the most enchanting garden.

"We can't take your body. That will have to remain on the hill. But your mind can come with us – I'll link it to mine! Just agree and you'll see through my eyes, and hear through my ears. The thoughts of those we encounter will be open to you. We can even share memories!"

I did agree. Who wouldn't?

And for a time I was Puck and Puck was me.

It was the most, mind-boggling dream-experience; and even after they had dropped me back at the hill – to reunite with my body, enough of our link remained so that I could keep some memory of it.

Meeting Maeve afterwards was such good fortune. She helped me make sense of the "Mysterious!" I'm not the first person she has helped. She has met other children in the past but I, alone, have seen her dressed as a fairy!

Maeve encouraged me to think of my dream as a story and to preserve it in written form. Talking, remembering and writing are not just effects of a dream but a way of understanding it.

I wrote it quickly! Before the memory of it faded from my mind. Now the mental link has gone forever, but I'll never be able to top visiting the Garden – or being a fairy on Midsummer's Eve.

4. AN AWED ENCOUNTER IN A DREAM

Sitting on horseback, Puck inserted his hand inside a cloud and withdrew it holding a bowl. Dipping his face into the bowl he made a succession of slurping noises, before emerging with his face all covered with cream. Licking his lips and turning to his fingers, Puck finished his meal of cream.

"Mind you don't drip any of that on my coat. Be sensible and save some room for the feast." The slurping continued so Nebula did too. "Flying to and from the Garden is bad enough. But when you have a fat fairy on your back..."

"I promise not to break your back, old thing. But I won't be eating. I'm on a mission and I want a word with the Queen!"

The Queen had swapped her carriage for a globe of light. The fairies, astride their horses, formed rings around the globe, as if they were circling a planet. The globe floated with the Queen inside. Puck concealed himself on the edge of the ring formation.

The most wonderful part of the unseen world is the Garden with Many Names. Every plant from every garden exists here. But it grows larger, more abundantly and with more life. The very air in the Garden contains something wholesome and it commands all who breathe it to be free and seek their nature.

Herbs and flowers grow here. Enough to satisfy the wants of every bird, bee, or butterfly, they attract. Now, the Queen and her subjects are not mindless insects (but tradition can become instinct) and feeling the call to swarm, they had flown to its flowers.

Being part of their kingdom, it may seem strange that they did not dwell here on any other day; but in truth, they only gathered here on Midsummer's Eve.

Happily, for mortals, the most beautiful of Faerie's many gardens is continuous with the human mind; but we, mortals, seldom visit it, on any night or day.

During the ride to the Garden, my self was but the minutest speck; Puck's mind was so big, I felt dwarfed by its concepts. A multi-coloured explosion of light was my first distinct experience of the Garden. I re-emerged to find I had fairy senses, and what interested me most was the horses' manes.

The horses twinkled their manes! And I saw colours that I could not name.

I became aware of talking and felt myself sinking into a blissful drowsiness; I pulled myself back before I was carried too far under, I intended to be present throughout my dream. The talking continued but I could recognise the voices now. It was Nebula and Puck.

"Can't we get closer to her?"

"Nay, my neighing friend, I want to stay hidden."

"Don't jest with me. We both know you serve the royal court."

"I served King Oberon and Queen Titania. I was more than a court jester to them. But I don't expect a horse to remember either of those two."

"Not true. I remember Titania. She rode my mother to her dances. I haven't seen her for ages, Puck. Did something happen to her?"

"I wish I knew. It puzzles me how we ended up with Mab as Queen."

Indeed, if there had been a contest between the new Queen and the old, Puck would have bet on Titania as the victor.

The ring they were part of was moving now. And within minutes, it had broken up completely. Soon there was no more formation to see. The body they had encircled was gliding downwards now and they followed in its path of descent.

Puck's words had made Nebula even more eager to be near the Queen. And as soon as a gap appeared – in the mass of bodies all around them – she took them as close to the globe as she dared. They could both see the Queen now and Puck's "Ho, Ho, Ho," was far from his lips.

Yes, the Queen had eyes as blue as the sky but Puck had seen bluer eyes in a fairer face. Titania had worn the same crown and the same leaf-berry-shell jewellery, but she had never needed them to show she was Queen.

Inside the globe, the Queen raised a flower to her face, seemingly, to smell it. Somehow, Puck had the impression she was doing something else.

"I wouldn't eat that," snorted Nebula. "It's got a funny colour."

"Why! It's a *Black Rose!*" cried Puck. "And it's my belief it talks to her and it speaks in the *Child's voice!*"

Mab stepped out of the globe and watched as it ascended back into the sky. She knew it would remain there until she needed it again.

The voice inside the Rose was angry. There was some agent in the air more powerful than its words. With the Rose silent, Mab felt as if some part of her was missing. The Queen was feeling the influence of the Garden; its effect on her was like medicine, but what patient likes medicine!

'Is this what it's like to be free? Where has the voice gone? Do I want to be free?"

A barrage of sights, sounds, and odours struck her senses and it took a while before they were recognisable. Everything was new and unexpected as she experienced them anew.

Hares had never boxed as madly (as they were doing now). The nightingale had never sung so heart breaking a song (as it was singing now). And the colours on the peacock's tail had never shone in such a dazzling splendour.

Now, Mab had seen (and heard) all of these things before. She was old enough to have grown weary of them. The Child understood her emotions, that's why listening to her was a dark pleasure. But the Garden was not a wearisome place and it made her feel uncomfortable that she felt so differently here.

Tonight the sensory force of the Garden seemed at its strongest. Now lambs, goats, and deer greeted her. Rabbits leaped and flashed their tails (knowing the Queen watched them chase). The Garden was hers to experience, undisturbed, before her people came down from the sky.

Later: Mab's people have come down! They're feasting, dancing. The people of Faerie are drinking nectar.

A gold-skinned maiden dances with a muscular lord. He bows his antlered head to her and swings her round and round.

Weird Talking Flames hover at the shoulders of delicate, ethereal women, while, earthier, green-skinned, cobbler men jest with a Knight who has discarded his shoes.

A bodiless fairy is only knowable to those who come upon him as a shiver down the spine.

Mab was puzzled. Everyone should be here. But someone seemed to be missing.

Sitting on a beehive felt different from sitting on a throne in Fairyland. The Queen was reluctant to make comparisons so she focussed on her subjects instead. This was a night for decision-making and one of those seen would soon be King or Queen of the Garden.

There is some trick here and I suspect magic.

No one had ever dared play a trick upon the Queen before. It was unthinkable. This was the most bizarre of all the novel experiences that had occurred to her that night. Her world had been grey and unchanging but now...

"I am full of questions," she sighed. "And who have I got to answer them?"

No sooner had she spoken than a hairy, pointy-eared man appeared before her doffing a floppy, three-pointed cap. Mab smiled at the gaudily dressed figure as it took its bow.

"I see through those Fool's clothes and see the Puck within.

A Puck that dares fool with the royal mind had better have an explanation ready for his Queen."

"Why would your Fool trick you? My concealment of myself is only so I can surprise you. I seek no harm to your mind...quite the contrary."

"Then my mind is not being influenced?"

"I didn't say that."

"Come, speak plain, Fool. You mean Siofra: the *Child*!"

"Yes, evil Siofra, the Voice of the Speaking Rose!"

"Evil, tut, you know the legend, Puck. It belongs here. This is its home."

Puck was kneeling now and the Queen hoped that fearing her, he would hold his tongue.

"Rise, Puck. You don't have to kneel to me. The Child doesn't want to harm the Garden. And I wouldn't let her. She just wants to see her father's resting place."

"Then she'll be disappointed. There are no bodily remains now, as we both well know... Besides, the one called Lone Sarsen doesn't rest. He is the most *alive* dead person there's ever been."

"Don't you feel for her? Her father never explained his plan to her. Imagine her shock when she saw him make a copy of his skull. You and I are aware of the spiritual meaning of the *Skull*. We appreciate its role in ceremony. It's a Wisdom Head and an enlightenment device. But the only meaning the Skull had for her was her father's mortality. Of all the things her father created; this was the one that was most beyond her comprehension."

"It's beyond my comprehension why you'd help her return. She's the most embittered of exiles. So changed from what she was. I fear for this garden! Siofra so hates the Garden she will destroy it! I'm not even confident that the Skull can save us."

The Queen flinched. If he continued on this path, she would become angry and she could always accuse him of treason. But anger seemed so difficult here.

"Some say she helped Lone Sarsen create the Garden."

"And more reliable legends claim otherwise. Siofra didn't come before the Garden. She was one of twins: granted life here in these very surroundings."

But Puck had not come here to talk about legends.

"I want the Rose!" he cried.

Mab looked down at her hands in alarm. They were empty. She was about to accuse Puck when she remembered where she'd hidden the Rose. Her hand trembled as she lifted the Rose from her lap.

It doesn't speak to me here. Why doesn't it speak to me here?

"Give it to me and you won't ever hear its lies again."

"You want me to hand over my Rose!"

Puck nodded his head in answer. Mab realised then the power a Fool has over his Queen. Defiance would not do so she replied with a plea, "Without my Rose, I would be nothing. Do you want me deaf and blind?"

"Better, deaf and blind than see the world distorted."

The Queen's lip trembled. Puck wondered if he had gone too far.

"There is no distortion." Mab tightened her grip on the Rose. "The world looks black to me! Just like this rose."

Puck had to stop himself from reaching forward and plucking the Rose out of Mab's hands. He knew that if he removed it against her will, her mind would remain in the shadows.

"Your world has changed now has it not? Look! The flowers are brightly coloured again. There's space in your mind now, so fill it with the hum of bees and be happy."

The Queen remained silent.

"I am a fool, your majesty. Only good, for scaring the country folk, they love and fear their silly Puck. But being so silly, I could never believe *that* voice. And the Rose could never survive contact with my hand."

The Queen had her eyes closed now. But was she listening?

"These new feelings and sensations don't have to leave you when you leave the Garden. You can feel alive, Mab. Don't you want to feel alive?"

The Queen remained silent and then she spoke.

"Give up my Rose! Give it to a fool, never!"

"Then you leave me no choice. I shall call upon the power of my mortal helper!"

Puck's mortal helper did not stay passively observing for long, he called me and urged me to take possession of his body, I was to step out of the audience watching the play and stand on stage in the centre of the spotlight. Puck hovered near the surface of consciousness, while I spoke to the Queen. (Knowing I looked and sounded like a male of her race gave me the confidence to begin).

"You're pardon, Ma'am. It's Avery Smith. This Garden is a wonder to me. And I know you've been feeling the wonder of it too. But Puck's right, that Rose of yours gives the pair of us the creeps; so please, if you don't want to give it to a fool, give it to a mortal instead!"

"Insolent child! You dare to come here and speak to a Queen of Faerie! My rose must be truly precious, if so many conspire to take it from me. Be gone! My curse on you, Avery Smith! May you never come back here, while I am Queen!"

We had failed. I felt pity for the Queen.

The awe she aroused in me made it easier to forgive and understand her words. Surely, her curse couldn't keep me from returning to the Garden. I made sure to take one long, last look at her, just in case her words had any such power, before descending below.

The candidates stood outside the cave mouth. One had already entered the cave to face the Skull. The others waited their turn outside. There were seven of them. All mortal-born youths. They had not chosen to be "taken" but this was all right, as they were repeatedly told they were wise clever youths. They had grown up in fairyland and had lived like heirs to a great kingdom.

It was an honour to participate in the ritual inside the cave.

The boy stood at the back of the row. Waiting.

He knew mortals were a necessary part of the ritual. Only a human could control the memories and powers of the god-like Lone Sarsen. Only a mortal could survive the intense and all-consuming feelings of bliss that the King or Queen of the Garden must feel.

A fairy would burn up too quickly and would never reach the end of the twelve-month reign.

Choosing the Monarch was an annual event. To wonder what became of the old Monarch was only natural. Transcendence was his guess. (You could not go back to normal life after being King). But knowing the truth would not help him. Or alter his desire to become King.

The man in the green loincloth had made his fate seem more predictable but it still depended on his actions. There would be a question asked before the Skull and he must answer.

"Do not answer with words," warned Puck. "But look at the Skull as if you had never seen one before. And when you *see* what is before your eyes. You will be able to answer the question and pass the test."

How long the boy waited, he could not say but enough time must have passed for the other candidates to go before the Skull and fail.

He could feel the Skull reaching out for him. He was the last one left. It was up to him.

Puck would be the last fairy to leave the Garden tonight. Clad only in a green loincloth, his body hair was visible and there was enough of it to reveal that almost all of him was animal.

The Garden needs a strong king to protect it, thought Puck. *That foolish Queen is doomed. We must be ready for the Child.*

When the King emerged from the cave, there was no mirror, natural or otherwise, to show him the change in his appearance. He did not need a mirror to know his skin was faintly green. But did he realise what had happened to his face?

Puck could feel the power radiating from the boy's body. He imagined this must have been what it was like to stand before the living Lone Sarsen. But when had the Lone Sarsen ever worn a mask? Th*at's no mask*. Puck corrected himself. *You can remove masks.*

The boy must have sacrificed much to become King but it would be an insult to pity him. He was still the same boy, though changed by the addition of inherited memories; the boy derived his power to protect the Garden from those undying memories. This made him more than an heir that identified with the original. When necessary he could even become Lone Sarsen.

But the Queen was too much changed and for the worse. The Child's mind was a living mind and its relationships were parasitical. It secretly wanted more than to coexist with the Queen's mind; it sought her destruction!

"Do you want to see your face?" asked Puck. I can conjure up a looking glass."

The King shook his head.

"What happened in the cave? I know about the ritual. But what was it like for you."

The King placed his hand on Puck's head and Puck saw what had happened.

Earlier: emerging from the narrowest of passages, the boy came out into a large underground cave. The cave was almost as dark as the warren he had come through but at least he was able to stand. Candles flickered in lamps on the walls and the smell of incense grew stronger as he neared the centre.

He bowed to the Queen. A slight nod of the head was her

only acknowledgement of his arrival.

The Queen stood on her dais above the altar. The altar had big magical signs carved on the front. When one of them moved, the others whispered.

A dark cloth was draped upon the altar's surface. Upon it lay the Skull. Fireflies danced in its eye sockets. A mist about its mouth created the illusion of breath.

The boy knew this wasn't the skull Lone Sarsen had been born with. It was his Wisdom Head. It had the power and wisdom of the magician that created it.

The Skull had called the boy to it. And the boy had followed the voice of the long-dead wizard!

The Queen made him wait in silence before asking him the question.

"All fairies know that Lone Sarsen created the Garden. But can a mortal tell me what Lone Sarsen did, after creating the Garden?"

It was the Queen's turn to wait now. She wouldn't wait long. Quick! What was his answer?

Puck's words came back to the boy. He must see the Skull as a new thing. There are many possible things a skull could be. And none of them meant death. A skull is just a braincase. He had one too, and he was still alive.

The Queen repeated the question. The boy tried to remember the rest of Puck's advice.

"Answer child," the Queen interrupted his thoughts, "please tell me in words."

But he mustn't answer in words. The Queen was trying to trick him. But if he couldn't answer in words... that left actions.

The boy stared hard at the Skull looking for a clue. There was something special about this skull. It was looking very pleased with itself. It was grinning as if something wonderful had happened. As if it had made something good.

The boy saw the answer. He laughed and became King.

The night is almost over. Even we must leave. Both horse and rider are aware I am about to wake up.

Puck licks his fingers anticipating a creamy meal among the clouds. Nebula resists the temptation to look below (so she does not see the Garden at play). Goats, deer, lambs, and rabbits, take notice of their new King, then return to their games. The Garden has its protector again; he will love them and nurture them. They play without fear.

Must I awake? Must my last sight of the Garden be of the King?

No mirror prepares the King. He has no forewarning as his fingers touch his face to explore – a skull!

5. THE WISDOM HEAD

6 Trefoil Lane
Druids Ditch
Somerset
Twenty Seventh June 197-

Dear Maeve
Thank you for making friends with me on the hill. I didn't take in all you said to my parents, on Monday, but whatever you told them must have worked. Because they weren't as mad with me as I was expecting.

They have given me extra chores around the house and instead of going out after school, I've had to stay in and do my homework instead.

You took the fine weather with you when you left Druid's Ditch, Maeve, and it's been windy with showers here ever since. The sun has only just come out, today; it must have been cross with my parents for punishing me.

I woke up happy and practically bolted down breakfast, eager to go meet Jimi Flynn. I was looking forward to going to school with him instead of Mum.

I had my coat half on when a note shot through the letterbox and fell onto the mat. As it wasn't in an envelope and being too early for the postman, somebody must have shoved it in by hand. The note was from Jimi Flynn and it began with an apology.

"*We couldn't wake you, Avie. (No matter how hard we tried.) I had to get home. So Bobby took me and said he'd come back for you later...*

"*I've been thinking about our friendship, Avie. I'll be twelve soon and I'm growing out of the things you like doing. You see, I don't want to play our games anymore. It's all very well making up stories (when no one has a clue what you're up to) but you've been telling other people what we do now. And I'm getting so much ribbing from the other boys.*

"*I still like you, Avie Smith...*

Well, I was so angry and upset I crumpled up the letter and threw it on the floor. It has my tearstains all over it now. But I'll keep it to remind me of Jimi.

At least I still have Bobby.

It makes me sad to think how much Jimi is missing, just as the magic is starting!

I know it's only a matter of time before we'll be friends again. The lovely garden I saw in my dream is proof of how good the world can be and the world must be good to have such a lovely garden in it.

And no, Maeve, I haven't returned the piccolo yet. But when I do return it, I'll have some questions for Bobby.

Yours with love

Avie xx

P.S. I have started a dream journal just like you suggested but it makes for dull reading. The Garden seems always out of reach, even when I sleep.

I admit Jimi and I have played games and pretended in the past. But my dream was not "pretend." It was a Garden experience. How many I've had, I don't know, maybe more than one, but when I look back upon my feelings; when I saw the gulls soaring above the promenade, maybe that was a Garden experience too.

The elusiveness of the Garden is no excuse for wanting to keep the piccolo. I can't play it. Bobby can. And it's only when he plays it that the Garden seems within reach. So on Thursday 4th July, I went straight from school, to Wheatley's Farm, with a present for Bobby in my school bag.

If Mrs. Wheatley was surprised to see a girl calling on her lodger, she didn't show it. Letting me inside she directed me up the stairway, then returned to her kitchen at the back of the farm. I wondered if Bobby was in his room and I thought what a surprise it would be for him to see me.

I went up as quietly as I could but just before I reached the top, the stair creaked and gave me away.

Bobby opened the door, "You've come at last, Avery."

I don't know what was more surprising to me, his knowing I would visit him or the room he was sleeping in.

"The Wheatleys are into amateur dramatics." Bobby grinned at my astonished face. "I know it's OTT but it's the coolest of bedrooms."

The room was OTT, all right, but the props and the costumes (which were the true occupants of the room) were kind enough to allow us some space in the middle. Bobby sat on the edge of his bed while I stood waiting. Then remembering his manners he pulled a chair out from somewhere and I sat down.

"Have you seen Mrs. Wheatley try to do Lady Macbeth? It's funnier than Mr. Wheatley's Captain Hook."

"Oh, of course, Avie, you've lived here longer than me. So they're not good actors?"

"There's more ham in them than in Father Giles of Ham," I replied laughing.

"This wasn't always a bedroom, you know."

"It looks more like a store room than a bedroom, Bobby."

"It's still full of stuff! I don't have any old mirror, wardrobe, or clock, here. I have the enchanted mirror from Snow White. My wardrobe goes into Narnia. And the clock that wakes me up comes from Neverland. And the skin of the very crocodile that swallowed the clock, hangs on a nail on the bedroom door, there!"

"I'd love to sleep in a place like this. But, then again, isn't it a bit spooky? Isn't that a coffin over there?"

"That's no coffin. It's a treasure chest!" Bobby put on a pirate's voice.

The chest was as real as Bobby's pirate voice. It was wood though and had metal studs and hinges so would look good on stage. The chest lay in a dark corner of the room next to a map and a pirate's hook. There seemed to be something else there, too. I strained my eyes and saw...

"That better be a prop!"

"Can't you tell a real skull, Avie?"

"Ha ha, thanks for scaring me."

"But surely you're not frightened of skulls anymore – not after you've seen?"

Not after what I've seen, what does he know?

I was just about to ask him when the bedroom door flew open and Mrs. Wheatley barged into the room. It may have been rude of her to enter without knocking but Bobby has little interest in manners and we were pleased to see she was carrying a tray.

Mrs. Wheatley wouldn't dream of leaving until she had seen us drink tea and eat cake.

She was obviously curious about me and seemed to be one of those women who couldn't resist gossiping. Always wanting to find out more about Bobby, I was happy to listen to her.

"This has been the only decent home I remember having, Mrs. Wheatley. Not including my time with my father, that is"

"I'd have a word or two to say to that father of yours. If only I knew who he was. You're lucky it was me found you. Some other family would have turned you off their land as a trespasser!"

Bobby gulped his tea and bit into his cake and even he must have felt embarrassed as the farmer's wife went on to describe the "discovery" in ever more humiliating detail,

"What a shock I got going into the barn. You don't expect to see a young man, all naked, sleeping under the hay. You wouldn't let us near you at first. Talking nonsense you was. And you were clutching the strangest things in your hands."

"Was he holding a piccolo?"

"How did you know that, my girl? And he had something else with him as well. Something that you normally only see when you get your fortune read ... 'That will be perfect for

Wizard of Oz' I thought ... It looked so authentic. Just like a crystal ball."

"I still don't remember ever having it, Mrs. Wheatley. Are you sure you didn't imagine it? After all, you've looked everywhere for it."

The farmer's wife looked as if she wanted to search the room, there and then, and I was secretly relieved when she suddenly remembered she'd left something in the oven, and left the room. However, maternal she acted towards Bobby she didn't seem to believe he was speaking the truth.

Thanks for reuniting us. She would like to thank you too."

She was the piccolo and I felt a thrill of excitement, I was about to be thanked by the music of fairyland. Bobby's next words brought me down to earth.

"I'm not going to allow her to go all magical again. Can't have us both getting lost in dreams and visions, you can't always get out of them."

Bobby's talk of visions didn't mean he disbelieved my dream. He couldn't deny what he had also seen. And he had more information to add to my account.

Remember the man who claimed to be Bobby's father? Well, he was no longer a mystery. He'd wanted Bobby to try his hardest to remember him.

Now, quite unknown to me, Bobby has been spending hours and hours, in this very room, trying to awaken the past. He's been listening to music whilst doing this. And it seems he's been successful.

Bobby knows exactly who the kind old man is now.

Once back in Bobby's memory ... other memories ... memories of the Garden followed.

"And that's why he gave you the piccolo. So that when you played it, you'd see ... what we've both seen. But who was he, Bobby? And where is he now?"

"Can't you guess, Avie?" Bobby walked over to the chest,

removed something from the top of it, and came back with the skull. He dropped the prop into my hand then said, "Remember the King of the Garden? The boy who *saw* the Skull's grinning as a creator's laughter and passed my father's test with jollity."

"Your father was the Garden's creator, Lone Sarsen!"

I almost dropped the skull.

"Have you ever started to say something only to have a friend finish your sentence?"

"Well, of course. Who hasn't?"

"Well, it's not only sentences that get completed in this way. A dream. A story. A creator's plan for his creation. Some thoughts are timeless. Some of our conversations eternal!"

What was that about getting lost in dreams?

"Lone Sarsen's parents ... my grandparents ... were the strangest couple. He was an arch druid and she was a fairy. This gave my father an advantage over other wizards. He was able to slow down the aging process (a wizard's top goal then) ... but longevity is not immortality."

"You can't avoid death, Bobby."

"The alchemists tried to. Did you know that some of the alchemists created 'heads of wisdom?' Those bronze heads really were wise. They could speak!"

"They only teach us chemistry at school."

"My father made the earliest known head. He was experimenting with mist and moonlight and the end-result of his experiment was a replica of his cranium and lower jaw. This was superior to the later alchemists who could only animate metals like brass."

This is as strange a tale as any dream.

"The 'Skull' is not the name I'd choose for my immortal head. On some level, others see its meaning. They can't help it. They see a skull. They know this creation of his mocks Death. The more enlightened might see a face or at least a smile.

"My father only allowed himself to die, when he had given the Skull his powers. His life hasn't truly finished, Avie. He still looks after us ... and the Garden!"

"That's a nice thought, Bobby. I hope it's always so."

"While the King wields *his* power to protect. And the Skull grins like the wisest man alive. While *his* name is still spoken with awe. And *he* acts through his agents: a grinning skull and a boy-king! It remains so."

Now, one of the powers the King of the Garden has is mental projection. That's how Bobby was saved from perishing on the streets after running away from home.

When the King knew Bobby was on the streets he created a vision of Bobby's father. Bobby didn't know that the kind old man (who seemed real) was really memories projected from the King's mind. The projection was no mere illusion; however, it was fully tangible! Alas, the illusion was short-lived; for once Bobby was safe the kind old man left without saying goodbye.

Bobby didn't need pity. "Better to be cared for by my dead father (even if he was an illusion) than be hated by a couple that never wanted me."

"No one hates you, here, Bobby. But If I'm honest, I feel the same as Mrs. Wheatley does. I'd like an explanation from your father. If he still looks out for you, how he could have let his own son be taken away and left with that couple."

The sadness that came into Bobby's eyes was my fault. What foolish words. How could Lone Sarsen explain? Bobby might be right to question when a life finishes, but that doesn't change the fact that his father is among the dead. So long dead, he is now a legend.

Days passed and I realised I wasn't missing Jimi. I never asked Bobby if he missed Jimi. Doubtless, we will miss him later (if he continues to keep away from us).

Bobby's the friend in my life now, and a lot of our time's spent talking about the Garden.

Bobby suggested that I should write about the Garden, and even attempt to draw it!

There is one more incident to record before I finish this chapter. For the past few days, I have been following Bobby's instructions to "enchant my recorder" and "to capture the singing of birds." I get up early before Mum and Dad are awake, and I go down to the lawn of our little front garden where I leave my recorder out on the grass.

I have been doing this for two mornings now and I left it there this morning for the last time. The recorder will somehow absorb the bird song and I should be able to conjure it up again, whenever I play. In time I might become as good as Bobby and then maybe I will see the Garden.

I have just been out to the front lawn to retrieve my recorder. There is no sign of it. It's gone!

Little did I know then, that a mysterious, yet powerful individual had been observing me each morning, or that she included me in her plans! She needed my help and had few scruples how to get it.

Her story follows next (as heard from her own mouth).

6. SHEELA TELLS HER STORY

If any other girl had asked me to take up this tale to continue it, I would have sent her packing with a curse. My curse is not to be provoked, believe me. But Avery Smith is the only child in our village not to run scared of me; and events that connect us make me part of this story.

Let me begin by introducing myself. My name is Sheela. I am a wise woman. And at the time Avie first came to see me; I was the White Witch of Druid's Ditch. A prophetess usually seen at the pier.

My look was traditional with wild black hairdo and heavily made-up face. I dressed in scarves and shawls, my clothes were either purple or red. To complete my look I perfected a "far-seeing" stare and kept an open pack of Tarot cards close by.

Now, I was no fraud at this stage. I could see the shadows cast by future events. And yet this hadn't always been so. The version of me that you are about to read about wasn't the least bit psychic. But I'm getting ahead of myself. First, I must tell you how I became the Witch.

The secretary was the plainest and most pitiful version of me. I'd like to disown her. But for a while she was me. She had no weirdness or mystical power. That would only come back when I came back!

Back when I was the secretary, I found it easy to type for hours. Much harder to make friends.

No one asked about my family and I was happier not thinking about them. There was no one to celebrate my birthday with me, so no reason to take any notice of what the mirror showed me. The absence of friends, family, birthdays, or mirrors left me without age.

But others saw me differently. After years of loyal service, my boss thanked me by firing me and hiring a sixteen-year-old girl to look pretty and type badly. Instead of getting another job straight away, I took a holiday in Devon.

Now, a witchcraft museum is a fascinating place to pass an afternoon or two. And it must have made an impression on me because when I came back from Devon, I had a pack of Tarot cards and some attitude.

After some practise, I was a good enough fortune-teller to convince people I could divine the future. I played the part of the zany Tarot card reader and decided to fleece the gullible idiots who believed in my foreknowledge.

I had never been to parties before and it was only thanks to my fake powers that people began inviting me. No man or woman wanted to kiss me – but they all believed I could tell them when a stranger would come into their life and kiss them.

My life before had been lonely, but peaceful but now I was starting to feel frustrated. I could see all these people having fun – fun that I'd never been aware of before and so hadn't missed. One of the partygoers called me a "witch" and I was happy with the label. (This was around the time when my predictions started coming true). Now, being a witch doesn't pay the bills and to save money I moved to a much cheaper house in the oldest part of the village. An old cottage with a thatched roof – stood all by itself – next to a rundown allotment with a graveyard behind it. Even this house was expensive to live in. I wasn't willing to ditch my tarot cards for a typewriter, so when I saw the advert for the job at the pier I jumped at it.

The woman who interviewed me was dressed even stranger than I was. She wore a crescent moon headpiece, had serpents tattooed all over her arms, and had a rather strange-looking earring in her right ear – which turned out to be a key.

"Back in touch, at last! Never thought I'd need an advert to get you to see me! You've dressed well for the interview, Sheela. You've got the job! Now let me tell you about it."

Only the Goddess Hecate would talk to me so.

Now, the secretary had a skill I wish I'd always had. Her filing was faultless and she never lost information.

The first half of the interview reacquainted me with Hecate. I almost laughed at the irony. I only became the secretary because my overloaded brain couldn't store all the centuries that I'd lived as a witch.

It soon became apparent that my job at the pier was "just a cover." I wasn't there to tell the future – although giving advice was part of the job description.

"I want you to act as my eyes and eyes. I try to leave the mortals to themselves these days but it still becomes necessary for me to act sometimes."

"Do you want me on the pier? I've seen the rides the kids go on. But there's no booth for prophecy?"

"The booth is there when it's needed. You'll only need one in summer. I expect you'll be working from home in the winter months. No doubt, some of your summer clients will visit you at home, too. Not everyone wants to be seen visiting a seaside sibyl."

As a witch, I would have an animal guide. Mine was a kittenish young woman with a cat's ears and tail. She looked like she was wearing a costume. If you didn't get too close to her, that is.

"Let me re-introduce you to Flim Flam."

Flim Flam purred with pleasure upon seeing me again. "Everything you've ever known is all up here." She pointed to her forehead.

"Thank you, Flim Flam," I replied. "You're better than my own erratic memory. I think there's enough space in my brain, for some of those memories you've been looking after. Just the important ones, you can keep the rest."

Now, this interview was not happening in the waking world. Hecate is the Goddess of witches and fairies. So a dream is the most likely place you'll find her.

In case you're wondering what is the difference between witches and fairies? There isn't one. If you appear young and you have power, they'll call you a fairy. If you look old and you have power – they'll call you a witch or a wizard, those in between have a variety of labels.

My second important meeting with Hecate occurred at the time of the full moon. Just over a year had passed in my new role and the only contact I'd had with the Goddess was some fragmentary dream messages that didn't make sense.

"What's wrong?" I asked.

A Goddess shouldn't look worried. If something can worry Hecate, I should prepare for the worst.

"We've lost the crystal! The child, Siofra, is about to break free!"

I looked blankly at Hecate. She seemed to be making a lot of fuss about a child.

"Hasn't she come back to you yet?" snapped Hecate. "What have you and Flim Flam been doing since I gave you the job?"

I resisted telling her that if she wanted me to remember things, she shouldn't have sent me to the pier. I'd had so many clients come to see me; the pier was in danger of collapse. You need solitude for memory work; many of my old memories hadn't come back to me yet because they were still in Flim Flam's head!

"You're the best of my warrior witches, Sheela. It's been true for centuries now. It was your idea to use the crystal. You sprang your trap and lured the Child inside. You stopped The Child sending nightmares to mortals by turning a divination ball into a cage."

"Didn't you just say this crystal is gone?"

"Correct. It was barely holding her prisoner as it was. I was going to ask you to make a new one. That's why I asked for the old one to be taken out of storage."

"Surely you didn't leave it unguarded?"

"It was guarded by Cerberus."

Even the secretary had heard of the three-headed dog guarding the underworld. She thought this knowledge had come from a document on Greek Tragedy. (Her first-class typing meant some interesting documents came her way).

"Three heads, no brain, it would make the mortals laugh if they knew how dumb he was."

Hecate's wisecrack failed to lighten the mood but it was pointless being angry with Cerberus. Whoever this Child was she was clearly powerful and could fool with the strongest of minds.

Hecate nervously fingered her key-shaped earring and told me all.

"The crystal is not such a great prison these days. As her long confinement ends, the Child is aiming for something worse than poisoning the odd mortal mind. She's aiming for a fairy mind. Mab's mind! Imagine Faerie's most beautiful garden with black flowers and a zombie Queen. What hope for mortals then? No childhood, imagination, or wonder for any of them!"

"I don't know why I should care about mortals. But the very young have never done me any harm. I'll be a warrior again."

"Good. While I seek the missing crystal, you must work! You must make a new crystal: consecrate it, bury it!"

"I'll bury it when the moon hides her face from our eyes. But when do we attempt transference? When do I dig it up again?"

"The crystal is to be above ground again, in time for the moon's rebirth."

"It's a good thing I'm well versed in moon's phases. You must find the missing crystal, Hecate. So we can have both crystals together, when it's time!"

The foot I held in my hand was restless. It belonged to a beautiful youth – who was obviously finding it hard to relax. It is my misfortune to make such youths nervous. After all, who wants a witch to tend their naked foot?

Bobby had turned up while I was preparing for the burial. Flim Flam had "helped" me with the crystal and while I appreciated her help, we both agreed she could roam free until needed again.

Please do not be mortal. Let mortal women look at other

faces. But, please, let me have yours.

A tall lad with longish hair most folks would have dismissed him as a simple country boy. He told me he was a farm labourer and that his employer recommended me as someone to heal wounds. He struck me as a reader of nature rather than of books. Bobby claimed his foot was paining him and was uncomfortable to walk on. True, it had minor bruising but his story that he'd hurt it falling from a haystack didn't ring true.

I applied ointment to the foot. Bobby trembled as I touched him.

He knows who I am. He wants me to know it.

Now, it is a rule among us magic folk that we do not form attachments to mortals. We can love (if you want to call it that) but only in the sense of loving life, nature, cats, or womankind. And if we break this rule of ours what happens? Hecate punishes us. Hecate is not vindictive She'll only punish out of duty, but she has her rules and reasons and she expects us to obey them. Any punishment will be swift, certain and it will destroy us.

This baby wizard knows too much to be a mortal.

I should have kept closer watch of the boy but holding his foot and looking at him was nicer than entertaining suspicions of his gaze. I could see no reason for him to keep looking around my cottage parlour, or stare into its corners, there was nothing hidden in them for him to see.

I decided to keep up the pretence I was a harmless fortune-teller, my gifts endorsed by celebrities who posed with me, in posters on my walls. None of that interested him. All he did was stammer; then withdraw his foot.

"You're not going," I said.

He nodded – still trembling – and I tried not to laugh as he put his left foot into the wrong boot. It never occurred to me to question why he should want to leave so suddenly. I was too busy with other thoughts.

"I see your foot is better now. What about thanking me. It costs little to make me happy."

"I thought your help was free."

"Not for you it isn't. I'm a woman behind these clothes. And you're not the youth you seem to be."

"I don't hold with witchcraft," cried Bobby – both feet in the right boots now and with the laces tied ready for him to run.

"These lips have never been kissed."

Bobby stopped trembling but when he answered, his lip quivered almost imperceptibly. "Well, they're not getting kissed by me!"

If I had the crystal near me, I would have thrown it at his head.

The boy fled and standing alone in my house, I felt hatred such as I had never felt before. The hatred did not become a lasting part of me and I can thank Flim Flam for that.

"The man who left," hissed Flim Flam (not bothering to come in through the door but floating through it instead). "He's got the crystal! And its place of concealment has been discovered!"

"How do you know this Flim Flam?"

"My informants told me."

"What animal shades have you been listening to?"

"Rat Shades, nasty things...but they're too scared of me to lie. They've been keeping an eye on the farm for me lately. That long-haired labourer has got them suspicious and as soon as they saw him come here they told me everything – immediately."

"The Goddess will be pleased. I am her best warrior and without even searching, I will have the crystal under my roof tonight. I dare not wait for the new moon, Flim Flam, but must bury the crystal as soon as it is night. And you, my feline friend, you can go hunting."

My part of the night's labour was successful but Flim Flam could not complete her task. She didn't even reach the farm safely and was lucky not to lose her tail. The baby wizard succeeded in keeping her away.

"It looks like a stalemate. I can't get the old crystal. And Bobby left without the new one."

I was curious about Bobby. Did his trembling and stammering mean anything or show the power I could hold over him?

He has a man's beauty and his own kind of wisdom.

I was determined to know more. If the Rat Shades could find out about him, maybe, I could too.

"He's not a thief, mistress. He's not the worst of men. But we can't trust him with the crystal. Or expect him to hand it over to us. The Rat Shades got sniff of the crystal about a year ago, Bobby was found with it on Wheatley's farm, and he's been keeping it in his room ever since. And the chest he keeps it in contains no pirate treasure!"

I wondered if the crystal had the power to transport itself. Cerberus was not a good watchdog. He never raised the alarm. Somehow, the crystal had come into Bobby's possession.

As a secretary, I was good at research. Now the secretary has awakened to her true nature, no man's secret is safe anymore.

When the night came for my crystal to be made ready for its captive, I had two visitors. Avery Smith spent less than an hour inside my cottage. Her visit wasn't unexpected as Flim Flam had picked up something of hers left lying on the Smith's front lawn.

Avie was disappointed that she couldn't have her recorder back immediately. But once satisfied that it was safe with me, and after agreeing that her friend was in the gravest danger, she made haste to the farmhouse to bring the imprisoned Child to me.

My other visitor was Bobby. The baby wizard!

No longer stammering or trembling. The sleeping spell that I'd put on him had worn off quicker than expected. Bobby was here, wide-awake, and I wasn't sure what to expect from him. Fortunately, he appeared to have come to his senses. He was almost friendly.

"You're right. My mind has not been my own. I can think clearer without her. I am better when she's gone."

"She? Bobby? Do you know who she is?"

"Only that her voice is familiar. She doesn't like it when I question her, or when I refuse to look into her ball."

"How did you come by it? Did someone give you the ball?"

He paused before answering: a soul-searching pause. Even my witchcraft couldn't have foreseen his wild reply.

"O, pity me, Sheela! I don't know who I am! Visions and guesses are all that I have."

"Trust me, Bobby. I know who you are. I've learnt stuff. And I'm convinced that your time with your father is the key to what's happened to you."

"My father! Do you mean the kind old man? The illusion!"

"You could have died on the streets without that illusion."

"You think he gave me the crystal?"

"When the crystal went missing he was the only one capable of taking it. He alone could act undetected by the Goddess. I suspect it was all out of kindness. Thinking he could save and heal the being within."

"But why give it to me? I couldn't look after it."

"Don't you know you have a twin? She is the one trying to take over your mind, Bobby. When the old man failed to heal her – he passed her over to you. Her brother!"

"She's the Voice!"

"You're shocked! You obviously have some memory of her."

"She's not easy to remember, Sheela. Not like my father or the Garden. I'm only thinking of her now because you claim she can possess me!"

"You've been through so much. You found your father – only to lose him. It's no wonder can't recall. You've had too much shock for your mind to deal with. And then there's that ball! The accursed crystal! It's robbed you of your identity!"

Bobby had arrived just as I had finished purifying my house

and body. Although my mind was busy anticipating the night's events, a part of me wondered how this man would view me, with my make-up gone, my hair no longer wild, clad only in a thin white gown.

Bobby was looking at anything but me (so even in lace I'd made no impression on him). Instead, his gaze fell on a ring of seven candles standing on my parlour floor.

I moved closer to him and lowered my voice.

"You see I'm not so old after all. And I must not feel old. For, it is a young maid's power that is needed tonight."

"Why do you hide your crystal from me, Sheela? Shouldn't we place it inside the circle?"

"I'm sorry, Bobby. It must remain hidden. It's not that I don't trust you. But you may not be as in control as you think you are."

I pitied my baby wizard and guessing that he would not mind, I took hold of his hands and pressed them between my own. We shared a look and I can only conclude that Bobby needed this contact too, because he allowed me to keep hold of his hands.

"But where's Avie?" he said. "I was hoping... hoping I'd find her here."

"That's strange! I'm surprised you didn't meet up with each other as she was coming back from the farmhouse. But she'd have hidden from you (if she thought you were coming after her). Still, why isn't she back yet?"

"You're forgetting the shortcut."

"But that's *through the graveyard!* She wouldn't. I warned her!"

Footsteps outside ... hurried footsteps ... Avie's?

Before I could open the door, Avery Smith burst into my cottage. Her face drained of blood and her body shivering with fright.

We helped her to a seat. "I'm sorry! I'm sorry."

Avie had returned empty-handed.

It took two cups of my best herbal tea (and my calmest voice and manner) to persuade her that the graves hadn't moved; and that the pit (she'd feared falling into) would have been a freshly dug grave: not the entrance to the netherworld! The Child had sent her some kind of waking nightmare and she'd fainted. On coming round, her first instinct had been to flee from the graveyard, and to make for my cottage. But when I asked her where the crystal was, her only response was to mouth the word "Graveyard."

Bobby must have left (during the confusion) leaving me no choice but to stay with Avie and to trust him. To lighten the mood I returned her recorder to her. I apologised for having taken it in the first place, "But how else would I have got you here?"

Avie was a brave girl. She must have recovered from her ordeal because she even managed to play a little tune on her recorder for me. Her playing was good for her age. Although she could not make life-like bird sounds yet.

"You'll get better with practise. But it's vital you pay attention to your dreams and recall them."

"So I'll see the Garden again, Sheela?"

"Seeing is overrated. Enjoy your feelings, Avie. That's the best advice I can give you."

Avie had other questions that needed answering and I did my best to answer them. She wanted to know if I believed Bobby was Lone Sarsen's son. This was harder to answer: for despite being eager to find out all I could about his past, I wasn't sure how well I'd succeeded in disentangling truth from myth. Bobby's puzzle was still missing pieces.

"He has to be someone's son so he might as well be Lone Sarsen's."

Avie agreed. Being a wizard's son raised Bobby's status and reflected well on her. But what if she believed he was a mere changeling? Would this diminish him in her eyes?

"I would love him whatever the truth turned out to be."

Avie knew all the signs of a changeling.

"They'd be cleverer than an infant should be. They might look old and strange. And that's one way you'd know they weren't just children. But that isn't like Bobby at all and hardly dignified for Lone Sarsen's son."

I have never approved of fairies taking mortal babies and yet Bobby had at least one trait of the changeling – his wisdom. Bobby was wise now. So if he was always wiser than other children that would have invited suspicion.

The old and strange part could never have applied to him (even on the brink of manhood he was fresh). But Avie was right about the indignity, as well as the misfortune, of leaving Bobby with humans who were suspicious of him.

"The Queen of the Fairies must have had a hand in it. It takes great power to lift a child out of his time. The Age of Wizards came centuries before the modern world."

"So Mab did it!"

I shook my head. "She lacks the power or the authority. I'm speaking of the Queen who came before. If Titania chose the 'parents', she chose without spite. Titania wouldn't have dared take Bobby from the Garden on a whim."

Avie thought she could see the flaw in what I told her. "But, that couple must have had a real child and it was taken. However nasty Bobby's 'parents' were they didn't deserve that!"

"Maybe there never was a *real* child. The couple might have been childless and the Queen gave them what they thought they wanted. Or maybe their real child would never have been happy with them and so switching babies was in everybody's interest."

Later: "It's getting dark in here, Sheela."

Avie noticed the change in the light before I did. The candles should have burned all night but instead their light was weakening. The circle (representing the whole of sacred creation) was in shadow. I relit all seven candles and once they were bright again, we could see what had been so easy to miss in the dark. The circle was empty!

I thought you were different. I thought you were beginning to like me. But by your actions, I see you're a thief. How did you even see it in my circle of candles? Where it lay obscured for no man to see. No man fears rejecting the secretary but how dare you reject the Witch!

Avie got to her feet and moved towards the door.

"Are you coming, Sheela?"

"Too right, I'm coming. We lost the old crystal because you went through the graveyard. Now I've made things worse by trusting a man. The new crystal is with Bobby. We're not losing another crystal."

When Avie first saw the gravestones, she tugged at my gown and gasped. They were just ordinary headstones now and didn't look capable of moving except for falling down.

A thin crescent moon threw down a spear of light in a sky clear of mist. Our heads were clear of dream mist too and we felt confident we were awake.

We have to trust our senses, Avie. We must. But never forget bad dreams like burial grounds. It is here they are at their most real.

I led Avie around the back of the church into the old graveyard. I stopped and asked the yews, the weeds, and the damp overgrown grass permission to enter.

The stones seemed eager to join the dead. Some were leaning earthwards. Some lay flat: one was broken. The writing on them was unreadable. We were soon to encounter reminders of Avie's dream. There in the furthest corner of this spot lay an open pit. We saw a patch of mist there too.

This was where we found Bobby. Frozen! Like a sleepwalker on the edge of the pit. A gleam showed the danger. He had only to open his hands and nothing would prevent the stolen crystal from falling into the pit.

"If it falls, she will have no more use for him. She'll order him to throw himself after it."

Avie seemed more concerned with the patch of mist than the fate of her friend.

"It's only mist, Avie. It cannot hurt us."

"You've not noticed it then?"

When I realised a schoolgirl had noticed magic before me, I felt a twinge of self-doubt. Could I really be trusted with her safety? The patch had doubled in size and density during our conversation. And it showed no sign of stopping. The mist developed into a vestigial body about the height of Avie.

The form started bulging at the top.

The bulge was the beginning of a rudimentary face that began featureless before the most horrible eyes and mouth appeared. I shuddered.

I could not un-see those eyes, or that deathly face with its cruel smile.

Limbs sprouted and grew hands and feet... a child's hands and feet to go with a child's eyes and mouth.

Bobby moved closer to the pit. Revealing glistening crystal fragments where his feet had been. No witness would ever know the precise moment when the old crystal shattered. It is only too probable that the Child broke free, whilst Avie was returning from the graveyard empty-handed.

The last time Avery Smith had stood near this spot, the Child had beset her mind with nightmares. No wonder she fled and dropped her charge.

I didn't want Avie focussed on failure so I gave her a task.

"Will he wake for you, Avie? We need the surviving crystal, back, if I'm to stand any chance of trapping that monster!"

"Wake up, Bobby." Avie urged, "Wake up!"

Too late, the Child laughed at us, demonstrating the power of her new body by leaping upwards and flying straight towards us.

She looks like Bobby! Bobby needs to wake up now! and see what his evil twin is up to.

A clock in the church tower struck twelve and the Child chose that moment to swoop over our heads. We ducked to avoid coming into contact with what felt like a freezing patch of midnight air. Laughing she performed several swoops before flying towards her brother's hands. But every time she tried to take the crystal from her brother, her hands passed through it as if still in their vapour form.

At last, she gave up and floating down to the ground alighted on the opposite side of the pit. Undefeated she made a beckoning gesture and the crystal came to life. With one abrupt jerk, it shot out of Bobby's hands. The shock of the ball leaving his hands was enough to wake Bobby. His first sight was to see it hanging unsupported above the pit.

Then he saw his twin.

There was no time for speech. I could only hope his mind was able to receive thought. Everything depended on Bobby's memories.

Look inside you, Bobby. See if there's pictures. I don't want anything physical from you now. But I need to be with you in your mind.

Images formed in Bobby's mind of his earliest years in the Garden. Bobby's image was not the important thing here. I needed the mental picture of his twin.

Evil cannot face its own reflected form. Evil hates innocence. Show the Child what she was.

Bobby responded and flooded his mind with images. The dismal graveyard could make no impression upon him now. The Garden was real to him and nothing else.

Then a most awful image appeared.

There was Lone Sarsen as the kind old man. He was showing the Child his latest creation. Her shock at the sight of the skull-like Wisdom Head was like an explosion in my mind. The images broke up with her cries of horror.

My contact with Bobby was lost. We only had words now. But I was still too shocked to talk. The Child wasn't shocked and spoke horror among the graves.

"You have shown me my awakening. I'm different now. I can bear the truth without screaming. That's just as well. For no one can hide from the truth in a graveyard!"

I ignored her words. I needed to do something ... something fast ... but what.

The little lights within the crystal were getting brighter. That meant ...

It's heating up. It's smoking, going to explode.

I closed my eyes. When I opened them, not only had the crystal been destroyed, the Child was gone. All that remained was a patch of mist sinking into the pit.

I hugged Avie to myself. And the three of us made our way back to my cottage. We were alive and sane. That was more than could be said of the Fairy Queen.

"What will happen to her, Sheela?"

"Her body will live, command and rule but without her personality. Mab will not be there! Not even to witness its possession."

I looked at Bobby. He knew this could have been his fate (had he not resisted his twin). His little acts of rebellion meant there was someone left for us to save. He thanked us, and then warned us of what he saw ahead.

"Weep for Faerie! All's over for the land! Soon all will be like the Queen. But her enemy, the King; he has godlike powers. And the will to protect the Garden."

"But that's little comfort, Bobby. Remember my dream. The King doesn't keep those powers. Will those powers get passed on now the Child is free? Or will the Child ruin things next Midsummer's Eve?"

Bobby had no answer to that.

"O, I won't want to see the Garden again, when this Queen returns!"

"We had reached the door of my cottage. "Take her safely home, Bobby."

I entered the cottage and shut the door.

The moment it was shut the outside world felt illusory, and I started questioning what had happened in the graveyard.

Why should a witch doubt magic? I'm longer the secretary. If her view of the world has come back, I must be tired.

A surprise knock at the door and all thoughts of the secretary were gone. I opened it to a heart-stopping sight. It was Bobby!

Naught parted us after that night. Bobby didn't give up his room in the farmhouse. Immediately. He remained bashful in his habits until autumn. This all changed in the spring: when, he told me he loved me. The Wheatleys let him stay on as a labourer. And come summertime, I would often venture to the fields to watch him working.

7. SHEELA FINISHES HER STORY

We rarely argued. And, yet, there was this one time when we had a different view on things and Bobby reconciled me to his way of thinking and I accepted what needed to be done.

We were arguing about Flim Flam.

Now, Bobby never liked Flim Flam. He was happy she kept away from him. I guess she reminded him of my past and the less witchcraft I did the less I needed her around.

Despite this, I cared for her. So I was really taken aback when he suggested her euthanasia.

"It's not as if she's a real cat. Let alone a person."

"She's not a figment, Bobby."

"But what is she? Is she an animal? An apparition?"

"She's Flim Flam. And we're not killing her!"

"But she's not alive in the same way we are. She's just a projection. And your mind is the source of the projection."

I felt so angry. I made accusations. How dare he try to trick me with words. He could leave!

When I calmed down, I found my own words.

"She purrs when I am silent. I can't purr. She doesn't get that from me. All I once was is in her purr."

"Stop thinking of her as real. She's a psychic projection!"

"Why do you hate her so? You're not bothered by the sight of tarots cards or bottles of potions. They're not threatening. They're not alive. But Flim Flim scares you. She's living witchcraft! She's my past!"

Oh, how I tried to explain to Bobby how important my pet was to me. I might not be much of a witch anymore but I still needed a cat.

"We owe her so much, Bobby. Without her, the life I once lived would overwhelm me. I would have to face all the Witch's memories."

"She's done a good job, I admit that. But how desperately we need those memories back now and the quickest way to get them is for Flim Flam to die!"

Sadly, I knew Bobby was right.

"I like who I am now more than I ever liked the Witch. But my past self has magical skills and knowledge and we have a Goddess problem!"

"If we are to survive Hecate, we must fight magic with magic. You must wake up the Witch!"

We both took comfort from the brave and almost serene way Flim Flam accepted her sacrifice. She was always eager to seek reunion with me.

So Bobby left us alone in the house for twenty minutes. The memories left Flim Flam's head and went back into mine. When Bobby came back, I told him she was gone.

Shortly after admitting we cared for each other, we decided to go on holiday to get to know each other better. We had a short break in Devon and while there, we visited the witchcraft museum.

While I was reminiscing among spell books, and cauldrons, Bobby found a broomstick for me. He was sending me up. We both knew I'd never use it. It remains of sentimental value though, and it takes pride of place in my kitchen.

Sometimes to amuse Bobby I pretend to fly on it. My Baby Wizard is fine with witchcraft when you turn it into a game.

Bobby's feet had been off the ground then, when he'd given me the broomstick in jest, but Bobby was serious and on terra firma now, as he proposed this latest test for my powers.

"Make it fly, Sheela. Make it fly!"

Despite repeated conjurations on my part, I could not get the broomstick to rise from the ground.

Flim Flam had sacrificed herself in vain!

Bobby blamed himself.

"I have cost you your magic and your cat. The Goddess sees me as a mortal man. That makes my love dangerous to you."

"Who wants her magic? My life is better now."

Words of bravado, Sheela ... words to spit in the face of your executioner. You know the penalty for rule-breaking. Loving a mortal is against the "Immortal's Vow." My one consolation, I have found this one man who can see something special in me.

Bobby held me to him defiantly. "You once said you were not so old after all. You were right, dear Sheela. It is a young woman who loves me. As it is a young man who loves you back."

We clung to each other – each needing the other's warmth.

Now the dread day approaches when I must meet Hecate and face her judgement. But I have won a young man's love. I don't want him to despair. Loving Bobby has made me happy. We should do what all couples do in the summer.

We swam under the pier and all around its legs. Then closer to the beach we floated on our backs waiting for the biggest waves to roll in and break over our heads. I liked being underwater as I could imagine my past pouring out of me and merging with the sea. When I emerged spluttering and laughing, I felt free.

It had been Bobby's idea to go swimming. He had chosen a spot that would have meaning for me. The water was colder and darker under the pier where I had once told fortunes in service to the Goddess.

The local hill, with its Iron Age remains, was meaningful to Bobby. Still exhilarated by our morning swim we danced all over the hill. But our mad dancing (on top of the day's exertions) brought on fatigue.

"Don't' drop off, Bobby. Let us not wander into Hecate's dream realm. The more awake we are the less power she has available to hurt us."

Bobby leaned in to kiss me. "I'll try to keep us both awake."

Healing Bobby had taken it out of me. So why be surprised when the cards got the future wrong? Or if an ailment got worse when the sick came to see me?

I had failed to see the signs of the Goddess's anger.

We waited in a shady spot near some trees. It was a cool place to rest and a good place for views. We'd see Hecate whether she chose to walk down from the hilltop or climb up from below.

"Will she come?" asked Bobby.

"I'm afraid she must."

"But I'm not an ordinary mortal. My blood is mixed. My father was Lone Sarsen."

"The Goddess likes boxes. You're in the mortal box. I'm in the immortal box. There must be no stepping out of our boxes. They must be kept apart!"

"Don't be tearful, Sheela. Don't let her win."

"Someone approaches."

We felt relief when we saw a villager climbing up the hill. I even had a smile ready for the middle-aged dog walker. Then I remembered dogs guard the underworld and Hecate is the Goddess of the underworld. Hecate spoke.

"Enough of the Art remains in you to heed my call."

"You mock me. You have taken my powers. Why?"

"Do you miss them, daughter?"

"I miss them less each day. But what gives you the right to take them from me?"

"Those who serve me must have hearts of ice. Those who follow me must be my Law."

Hecate looked at me accusingly. When Bobby answered her, it was as if my heart spoke through his mouth.

"Why can't she live as a mortal?"

"Your *male* addresses me. But I speak only to *you*."

"My male said 'Why can't I live as a mortal'. I ask that too."

Hecate laughed. "How can a daughter of mine ask me to make her mortal? Do you want to be a sick thing? Or end up a corpse? Be glad I still need you, Sheela. Give up this male and you can have your powers back. I'll make you stronger than before."

We answered Hecate in the only way we could. We turned our backs on her kissing passionately.

"Prepare for death. Pray that my fire destroys you. Pray that you will be spared the torments of mortality."

Hecate's wolf howl made us turn our heads. We saw her sharp canines glisten before the cold blue fire streamed out of her mouth.

Her fire is cold. Our hearts' blood is warm. It will be love that makes our bodies glow.

"Keep on kissing me, Bobby. Close your eyes, my love. When we open them, Hecate will be gone!"

We survived as I hoped we would.

Why couldn't Hecate kill her daughter? Here's my theory.

My love for Bobby meant the end of my magic and my immortality! The Witch began fading from me the moment I first looked into Bobby's eyes with love. Hecate was trying to kill a part of me that was in its death throes anyway.

An hour later, we were still on the hill. A reunited Avie and Jimi joined us, and they brought some food so we could picnic.

What wonderful memories children have! What a pleasure to revisit them. Avie had her Garden. Jimi had Bobby's piccolo!

Jimi's stand out moment was when he woke the spring! Jimi called the cuckoo out of Africa. Together they'd warmed the air.

Boy, bird, piccolo!

Leaving Bobby free to love me; now he'd passed the piccolo to Jimi.

Falling ill a few days later was revelatory.

My head was aching, my nose running, and I was sneezing and ruining my best handkerchiefs. What else could I expect from this mortal body? So when Bobby rushed in from the fields to care for me, I expected nothing else from his mortal heart. He'll make sure my illness passes quickly and then we'll see.

So the Witch's story turned out to be a love story. Its happy ending well deserved. I, Avery Smith, am also in a story. Dare I hope it ends so happily?

8. THE SONGS OF SPRING

Today is a good day. I had barely finished my Weetabix when a letter came through the door. As soon as I saw my name above the address, I smiled. Only two people would write to Avery Smith. My older friend Maeve doesn't write like a boy so it could only be from Jimi Flynn.

Absolutely everything about the letter was good. First, there was an apology and then the most wonderful story.

Now I'm not the only one to have a Garden experience! The omens for our future friendship look good, as this will be a new bond between us. I will go round to the writer's house immediately and we will be friends again.

Jimi Flynn must have hated the winter. The first winter in Druid's Ditch with no real friends – I don't call that gang of boys he hangs out with friends. How the endless winter days must have dragged. And while I was out chucking snowballs and sliding down the hill on my toboggan, he was doing something idiotic with his gang.

Bobby and I missed Jimi as much as he missed us. We didn't care if he dismissed our visions or denied Bobby's piccolo could make magic happen.

Yet it's funny how things turn out. Did Bobby know Jimi would come back to us if he appeared to him in a dream?

It might be better for Jimi to tell the story in his own words. So here are the best bits of his letter to me.

What a disappointment this spring has been! I haven't seen a single Robin yet. Let alone a butterfly. The trees think it's winter and so does the ground. My mum has been using the cold weather as an excuse to keep me indoors. She doesn't really like my gang.

Please let's be friends again. Life's not the same without you and Bobby.

But hey, it's my turn to be the storyteller now.

I went to bed last night not looking forward to the morning. I tossed and turned in a fitful slumber and woke up a few hours later to find Bobby in my room.

Wow, hasn't he changed, Avie?

I saw what looked like a young man at the foot of my bed. There was an aura of wisdom about this young man and he made me feel like a child.

"Jimi, I need your help."

You'll never guess what he got me to do.

"I cannot wake *her* from sleep. She needs *you* to play for her." He was talking about the spring. Just as humans may need an alarm clock, or a shake from Mum, to wake them up; so seasons need a reminder too.

I got out of bed and followed Bobby to stand before my bedroom window's frosted glass. We opened it to look outside, letting in biting cold air and neither of us liking the view.

"It's my fault its cold," confessed Bobby. "The cuckoo is in Africa still. It is her 'cuckoo' sound that is needed now."

I put on a dressing gown and we crept downstairs and out onto the lawn.

"I want you to have this!" Bobby handed me his piccolo. "Whether you keep her or not depends on how well you play. But I'm hoping you can take over my role."

It's funny how you can do things in dreams you'd never try in real life. I was able to play the piccolo and play it as well as Bobby. And so it wasn't clear if it was the piccolo or the bird (newly arrived from Africa) that was warming the air, with the lovely 'cuckoo', 'cuckoo' sound.

Have you ever seen one of those nature documentaries where they speed up the film and the seasons change in a few short scenes? Well, that's what it was like in my dream.

The dark night with its wintry weather departed the moment the rest of the birds arrived. First, I heard and then I saw house martins, cuckoos, and starlings.

"She wakes! Bringing garlic to our hedges and golden

catkins to our woods, returning to us in the crest of the courting male newt and in little leaf-wrapped eggs. See how she wakes! The piccolo is yours, Jimi. Play it and only part with it when you cease to be a boy."

When I first saw Bobby at the foot of my bed, I thought how wonderful it would be to be a man. But the piccolo gift changed things. What was my own boyhood but a gift? And perhaps there were better things to do with it than get into trouble with my gang.

Having played my role, it was time for me to go back to sleep. Bobby promised that in the morning when I woke up, all I dreamt would be true.

Spring would finally have arrived.

Mum gave me a wink over breakfast and asked me how I liked my surprise. I'd woken up to find the piccolo next to my football stuff and guitar. I was going to thank my mother but she shook her head.

"I didn't buy it for you. I found it at a quarter to four on the kitchen table! And I'm clueless how it got there. Do you know?"

She looked puzzled and rather than prolong her mystification, I started to explain my dream. And it was only while explaining it to her that I began to understand it. The "dream Bobby" may or may not have been in my room but the "flesh and blood Bobby" must have been in our house. Mum looked torn between relief and disbelief. She'd been keeping on at me about making up with Avie and Bobby who are always welcome in our house.

"So long as it wasn't that that gang of yours, I could have dropped my glass seeing it there."

My zombified Dad shambled into the kitchen yawning.

"Sensible people might think to take a glass of water to bed with them. Considerate people don't wake their husbands up by getting out of bed."

Mum buttered his toast and he took the plate from her still

yawning.

"Was the kitchen door open?" I asked Mum.

"Most likely. As your father never gets round to fixing things properly."

"Well if you'd come down earlier you would have seen our visitor. You must have slept through Bobby's visit!"

"Well, I'm wide awake now and ready for the spring."

9. AN UNSEELIE CELEBRATION

6 Trefoil Lane
Druid's Ditch
Somerset
Twentieth June 197-

Dear Maeve

I hope this finds you well. I must confess I am still in a state of shock over your news. It is a good shock though. I am so pleased for you. I only hope that once your baby is born, you will still keep a little place in your heart for your old pal Avie.

My mother is enjoying the psychology book you gave her and has begun to show an interest in my dreams. Only days before your visit, she and my father were still treating their own daughter as though she was just a teensy bit mad. (I have always been so careful not to tell them anything much about the Garden).

Mother's moods are much improved now, since we've talked about the days when she "feels down." I realise now I've got to help her and not get so scared. We will all understand ourselves so much better from now on.

The reason for your visit was not so surprising to me. You have always shown such a special knowledge of dreams, so it makes sense that you must study them as part of your job.

I can't thank you enough for helping me to understand my first, most wonderful dream (back when we met that Midsummer Day). You were just the fairy Queen I needed.

We are all waiting to see what you make of my "Case" when you finally write it up in the *Journal for Psychical Research.*

My father is constantly trying to explain Jung's theories to me. The talk around our dinner table is all about the Unconscious, and Jung's Archetypes.

My conscious mind is unique to me but not so my

unconscious. That's shared and contains images and ideas that turn up almost everywhere in mythical thought and dreams.

I don't know whom I have the most trouble understanding: Bobby or Carl Jung.

I wonder if I could ever grow up to be a scientist like you. (I'm not sure I'm smart enough.) So perhaps it would be better if I stick with my ambition to become an author instead.

I hope we will always be friends. But whatever happens, in our relationship, we will always feel connected through the Garden. When I remember your cheerful face and recall your gentle voice, I share your belief that the Garden endures timelessly and its complete destruction is beyond any evil fiend's accomplishment. But, Maeve, that belief of ours is about to be put to the test.

Yours with love
Avie

Have you ever had a false awakening? When you seem to have woken up but unknown to you, your body is still asleep and the unreal has tricked your mind? I had a particularly vivid instance of this on the 23rd of June.

I was impatient to get up that morning. Not to enjoy the sun but because Midsummer is the day when fairies visit the Garden. (And a lot must have happened in Faerie, in the twelve months since my dream). I was willing to take on any role the evening demanded. All I knew was that Avery Smith must be ready to play her part.

I never got as far as throwing off the sheets. Any notion of rising collapsed after sensing someone in the room with me. Something told me this wasn't my mother. The presence spoke and I recognised the Child.

"You may as well continue sleeping. There's no point you rising."

"You leave me alone or I'll scream for my mum."

"I can stop screams just as easily as I have stopped your

body's movements. I have come to warn you. Do not visit the hill. You're guide cannot get to you ..."

I was aroused now so should have been able to get up. As I couldn't, did this mean she was telling the truth? At least I could still speak.

"No good trying to scare me. Fear won't stop me or Puck."

"Didn't you hear what I said? There will be no guide. Don't look so disappointed. You surely don't want to see what I've planned for the Garden."

The Child came towards the bed and I swear her feet made no contact with the ground. My fear was that if she touched me with those icy-fingered hands I would die. But I knew better than to show fear. Even though my heart was racing as if it would burst from my chest.

"Ever heard of the Unseelie Court?" asked the Child.

"No, should I?"

"You saw the Seelie Court celebrating in the Garden last year... but those elves, pixies, leprechauns, and brownies have all gone. (I wonder what happened to them – can't have been nice)."

The Child levitated before me and once over the bed she lay herself facedown upon the air. She had me trapped beneath her, transfixed by her stare.

Close up, I could see a new resemblance between us - one that hadn't been there before. Bobby's twin was mocking me - changing into my double!

But she would never be me. I looked for differences.

My skin is not abnormally pale; my eyes are not darkened wells. She can't quite capture my voice when she speaks.

"The Unseelie Court rules Faerie now. We are the dark side of fairyland."

"Then thank goodness there's a light side. The King of the Garden will put a stop to you. You'll see?"

"If only he was still reigning. If only there was a mortal youth to replace him with, if only there was a fairy queen willing to test him for the role."

"You won't let me see the Garden again? Will you?"

She winked at me – displaying lashes ending in sharpened spikes. I was horrified at their closeness to my own eyes, but I kept mine open, out of fear of being at her mercy in the dark.

"Be thankful I spare you its ending. I have promised my court ... my boggarts and banshees ... that they will be the first to celebrate tonight."

I tried to calm myself by taking deep breaths but nothing would stop my angry outburst.

"Why," I screamed at her. "Can't you even answer why?"

"One day you'll laugh at your ignorant question. If I'm a disillusioned child then you must be the illusioned child, the one that can't imagine how anyone could serve DEATH!"

"You serve *DEATH*?"

"Yes! He is my master. I possess others in his name. He keeps me from resting and has promised me dominion over *Mind*."

My anger must have strengthened my body. I found I could rise. The Child retreated from the bed. I sat bolt upright and viewed her with curiosity.

"But you began in such a beautiful place."

"A beautiful place spoilt by the wickedest father. I was once, also, an illusioned child. Raised in bliss with blessings raining down on me; the day this bliss ended was when I saw my father holding his own skull. I saw grins on those two faces that made me drop my illusions instantaneously."

"You saw the Skull. It's not what it seems. Why do you think it's smiling?"

"You are not the only one trying to awake now. I may show myself to you here. But the greater part of me is in Faerie – in the slumbering form of the Fairy Queen."

The Child repeated her earlier warning then fell silent, her body sinking towards the floor. The floorboards rippled as her feet passed through it. Soon all that was left of her was her head.

Then that too was gone as it followed the rest of her through the floorboards.

Noon: I needed comfort after this nightmarish exchange and so I sought it in the company of the two I trusted most. We were in Sheela's cottage where she sang, chopping vegetables for a lunchtime soup.

I wondered at this, as she had never struck me as domestic before. But as Bobby laid out bowels on a chipped, white table set for three, I wondered if in time, I'd have to get used to such sights.

Bobby listened to my story without speaking. When I got to the bit about the Unseelie Court, I caught him smiling at Sheela.

Were they laughing at me?

"She cannot destroy the Garden, Avie."

Had I heard Bobby, right? Was he dismissing the problem?

I couldn't believe my friends' calm attitude.

"But she's bringing boggarts and banshees and all kinds of nasties."

Bobby carried on unperturbed. Sheela ignored me and stirred her soup.

"You can't destroy the Garden. You can only change its state. It will be different, that's all. That's all she'll succeed in doing tonight."

"It won't be a state for the better. Will it. It'll be worse."

"Things cannot stay the same, Avie. Not even the Garden stands still. All must change."

Sheela sniffed and sampled her soup. "Get some of this soup down you, before you go. It'll make you forget about the Garden."

I didn't taste a drop of her soup. (I don't think dream soup has any taste). Instead, I woke up.

Still in bed ... no one in the room with me. Enough light through the blinds for it to be early morning still.

If that wasn't the real Sheela and Bobby, maybe, I never saw the Child.

But what was my mind trying to tell me in that dream?

"The Garden doesn't stand still. It must change."

I can't ask Sheela or Bobby. (My dreaming mind may think of them as living in the village. But that's not true, anymore). The new life that beckoned them must have felt so important. That's why they left so suddenly.

I hesitate to say, I have Jimi. Is it safe to get him involved?

But should I – could I – face the Unseelie Court alone?

Jimi woke up with a temperature. His mother kept him in.

Looks like I only have myself to get in danger now.

It's nearly evening and I'm about to go. Then at the last minute, rain clouds appear over the village and I find myself confined indoors. Even if the rain stops, it will be too wet to lie out on the hill. And if the rain continues or becomes heavier how could I hear the gentle bird notes from my recorder? I go to bed numb. But after a few hours spent in self-pity, I remember the wonders of last year and it seems wrong to be unhappy now.

I will pray to Goodness and give thanks for the Garden.

My prayer's answer fills me with awe.

The Garden has come to my bedroom. She is here! She even makes my emotions speak.

"It is time! You have loved me dearly. You have sought me often. I reward you, Avery Smith. Now come with me."

My bedroom walls start to dissolve and all my familiar things fade away. Instead of being in my bedroom at home, I find myself in the Garden.

The first thing I notice is the heat. Fierce unrelenting heat. The source of this heat is a sun that has turned against life.

Its rays may as well be death rays, they do nothing but create desert.

The rabbits, deer, goats, and lambs that greeted the Queen of old, lie like wilted flowers now, their life force ebbing away, with no moisture for them to drink.

The next sensation is an ear-splitting cry. Woman dressed in grave robes wail like mourners at a funeral. I am grateful most of them wear veils. For unveiled their faces terrify. Blood red eyes with a single nostril and a single tooth.

While there is no music here, there is a kind of dancing going on among the members of the Unseelie Court as long-armed men with hairy bodies stumble, sway, and crash into each other.

The graceful, merry Seelie Court knew how to dance. But these bestial men and wailing women all move as if in pain. Then I see why. Their bodies are smoking and wreathed with flame.

Fire has come to the Garden. And with not a living tree in sight, she has all the death and decay that's needed to feed her.

Mab's body is untouched by flame and has a fairy woman's perfection still, but inside there is an all-consuming hate. There is a disillusioned child behind those eyes; and she has led her followers to burn on the Garden's pyre.

The Queen holds something in her hand. Its eye sockets and grinning mouth mean little to her, but the Skull is my last link left to my earlier dream.

The wise creator is here and he is still smiling.

For a moment, I am angry with the Garden. I feel like asking why she has brought me here. Her answer comes to me in a feeling: almost needing no words:

"You are here to help me change ... Avery Smith ... Girl with the Imagination of Wizards. Help me ... I must not be forgotten. I must not remain as this."

"But what can I do? I'm just a child."

"Will you receive me? Let me be part of you?"

"Yes. Be part of me forever. You're already in my heart."

"Do nothing now. Just watch and wonder. One day you will write my story. Then I will live once more – I look forward to the word-charms and visionary colours of my rebirth. I

predict you will have the most wonderful power, soon. It will be a gift you have truly earned. A power to recreate me, in hearts and minds to come."

And so I stay as watcher to witness the end.

The Child has restored the Skull's power of speech. But only to mock it. Still blind to any truth in its words.

Lone Sarsen speaks through the skull "Enough of this foolishness, daughter! This is no way to end your exile or to greet me. Let there be peace between us. You will never heal while there is hatred in your heart."

"If my father couldn't heal me, what chance do you have? Your fleshless face is a mockery of his visage."

"Flesh perishes but wisdom endures."

"My father had the eyes of a wise man. There was a healing power in his laughter."

"At last, you remember!"

"Then he shapeshifted into the opposite. Nothing could prepare me for the shock of seeing you!"

"My wisdom deserted me when it was most needed. I'm sorry, Siofra, I wasn't showing you death. I was showing you what I wanted to leave behind. My Wisdom Head was designed to bring enlightenment to the Kings and Queens that would one day protect the Garden. If my laughter was healing once; it can be so again."

"I will not know peace until this garden is destroyed!"

"Oh, Siofra! You sadden me. I see what's left of you. In that hollowed-out shell of a body you hide in. But you are not in the right mind to see me now.

"You are merely an illusion!"

"I am Rituals ... Memories ... Laughter! Not this skull, not boy-kings or girl-queens ... no space inside them, can hold all I am!"

Lone Sarsen must have guessed what Siofra would do next. As her fingers prepared to crush the skull, he did something she could not. He saw the funny side.

But his skull's wide-open grin was only the start. As the forces inside it made it quake and roar.

"Why are you laughing, you falsest of fathers? I am the Destroyer! Do not laugh at me!"

But laugh he did. And the laughter coming out of his mouth was a mighty wind of joyful defiance. The Skull shook and cracked until the whirlwind inside it, blew it apart.

Then nothing could stop his laughter now.

The wind took up the Garden and spun it like a spinning top, and then it shook it and shook it until it was atoms.

EPILOGUE

When wizards walked the earth, and the world was young, one of the most powerful of them all was a pacifist who lived in the West Country. His desire for peace wasn't shared by the warrior tribes that lived in Britain then. Nor was it shared by Roman soldiers threatening to invade from across the sea.

This not-so-young wizard was the most sought-after of magicians such was his fame at solving problems. But the demands of others sucked the fun out of being wise, so when he grew tired and needed escape he sought out the haunts of druids.

The Age of Wizards may have been full of marvels but it was also a time of invasion and conflict. In those troubled days, even druidic meeting places were under threat.

Could Britain really lose her wooded groves?

This possibility vexed the Wizard, as the last thing he wanted was to become warlike like the rest of his tribe. Being at peace was an essential component of wisdom. Remaining connected to nature was the source of his powers.

No longer an "ageless one," the long delayed years could take effect: most noticeably on his life force! Longevity potions were no longer helpful not now he felt fatigue for the first time in his life. But just a few moments alone in a sacred grove and the years would fall away from him until he was like a youth among trees. This was ideal, when he felt weary, near a grove, but was it necessary to go to a grove to feel young again. After all as a frequenter of groves, he had all the inspiration his imagination would need to satisfy his yearning for peace and renewal while out of doors.

The Wizard had a blessed beginning thanks to his fairy-mother. And although she left her "human marriage" when he was still a boy, she made sure to teach him all she knew of the Art of Imagination. Thus, the Wizard saw how the world looked in a twilight state of mind. And just like the fairy people, he saw only the thinnest of veils separating waking from sleeping. Once he knew the world's secret, he was ready to hear all that his mother would tell him.

She taught him the difference between dreams.

Small dreams are instantly forgettable, commonplace nonsense. Only big dreams pass through the veil. And if in future, he never saw her daily, or if sadly, they never saw each other at all, he could still enjoy visions of the realm called Faerie, if he attended to the rarer more revelatory dreams.

"I wish you many such dreams," she'd said to him. He knew then that she loved him. And that she didn't want to return to Faerie.

•••

He woke, one morning, before the sun. The early warmth and light told him the day would turn out fine. However pleasant the days were now; the year hadn't yet reached midsummer. Then days were at their longest. Then hordes of worshippers would descend on the sacred sites; and he would inevitably find his peace disturbed.

He remembered with longing how as a boy he was allowed his own space; and rather than watch the sunrise in a crowd of others, he would stand outside the sacred circle, on Salisbury Plain, and enjoy the solstice in his own way.

His tribe noticed the resemblance between their future wizard and the famous Heel Stone at Stonehenge: as both boy and stone occupied the point on the horizon, where the midsummer sun would always rise.

He made a resolution to make the most of the peacefulness now, and was about to go outside to see the sunrise, when he heard a girl's voice protesting by the entrance to his home. Moments later, she was inside – having almost fallen from the shove that sent her skidding upon his floor.

The girl didn't look Celt or Roman. And there was something about her, which made him wonder if she belonged in his time. She introduced herself as Avery Smith. His tribe had found her wandering by the hillfort and on noticing her strange clothes and her confused state; they had thrust her through the entrance of his conical home.

He bade her welcome and offered her some mead. She didn't like its taste much; but smiled at his kindness, politely putting the drinking horn away from her. She apologised for being in her nightclothes and asked him to pinch her. When he asked her "why," she said she'd been having lots of dreams and visions lately and this was the last place she expected to be.

He declined to pinch her, fearing the results would disappoint her.

"The Pinch Test proves nothing. Do you still do that where you come from?"

"Then how do we know what's real?"

It was then that she told him about a wise woman called Maeve.

"My friend Maeve is a very wise woman. She's been studying me and she knows all about dreams. She says there's such a thing as a false awakening. Once you have one you start doubting your sleep status. It gets confusing!"

"Enjoy the confusion, Avery. Dreams are wonderful. The best ones are stories. Tell me your story, Avery. And if you tell it well enough, I will know who you are. Make it exciting and inspirational, and as true as the legends I believe. Take your time and when you have finished, I expect to have tasted my finest horn of mead."

...

"Later: there was such a bitter taste in the Wizard's mouth when the girl finished her story, he felt a pause was needed before he next spoke.

That tale has a special meaning for me. But whatever atoms are, I don't think being shaken to atoms sounds good. I'm glad you survived, Avery. Methinks the winds were not purely destructive. They were purifying. Only breaking up what was bad. They spared you and blew you here - to a time and place of safety."

"But what of the place I've left behind? Is that really gone? Oh, don't answer! Just tell me a story instead. Are you a bard? This looks like a time when they still had bards. That's why I asked if there was a bard about when your people found me."

"I am a Druid. So I'm priest, wizard, and bard. After all you've seen and been through; you deserve a much happier tale from me than the one you told me."

The Wizard searched his memory for a story suitable for this child.

Nothing too violent or too saucy, but that left ... well, nothing.

Besides, he thought, it would be to follow her tale with something of his. (A tale's meaning needs time to sink into the heart). So being a virtuous man, he let habit take over and paid her a compliment.

"You're name is Avery Smith. That's a lovely name for a girl. If I had a daughter, I feel Avery would go well with the fairy names that I have imagined for her."

"And if you had a son, you could do no better than to name him, Bobby, after my friend."

"What a marvellous name. Like the boy in your story."

He was about to tell her his own name but she interrupted him.

"But where would you live? You can't all live here."

"But this is my home. It may be small but I don't want another."

"I'm not talking about a hut or a house. I'm talking about outdoors. Only a large garden would suit a wizard like you. And that's where I see you."

The girl smiled when she said garden. And once more, he couldn't help feeling there was something strangely familiar about the place she'd described to him in her story.

"That's funny, I already have a garden. Or a place that's like a garden."

"Is it near here? C'mon. You must show it to me."

He tapped his forehead. "It's up here, Avery."

The girl looked disappointed. "That means you can't show it to me. It's special. But only to you."

"I don't see why that should be."

"You are separate from me. That's why."

The Wizard was puzzled why she should think this; after all they had shared. Then a change came upon the kind old man and with a few looks, words, and passes of his hands, he cast his spell. Then he spoke. "How you leave here I do not know. Maybe you wake up in your bedroom at home. But you leave here changed from the girl you were. I make you a bard!"

She thanked him. Then he thanked her for the wonderful stories she would one day tell.

"Now you are a bard and a light-bearer. You and I know that nature is sacred and reverence is her due, that hearts forever young will always find eternity in everything; as a bard, your duty will be to awaken this feeling of enchantment in others. You must enthrall them as you have enthralled me. Share your stories, Avery, as I shall now share my garden with all who need it. Let the story of the Garden be an eternal one."

The Wizard hoped this would please the girl, once she realised what he intended to do. This girl had shown him. A wizard! How wrong it is to keep our most beautiful, healing thoughts secret. Since meeting her, he had named his future children and not only revealed his special place to her but had seen the Garden how she saw it: an enchanter's garden where child and druid bow their heads in awe.

The girl looked overwhelmed though. His words often had that effect on people. He didn't want her to feel uncomfortable so he asked. "Do you want to hear about my mother, Avery?"

"A wizard's mother, you bet."

"I suspect you already know of her. But I'll tell you anyway."

The tale of his tuition was such a long one he had to give up any plan to see the sunrise. Hours passed and the girl grew sleepy. He wondered if she would hear him to the end without falling asleep. He needed to make things clear to her before she left him, so he asked her this question.

"Do you know where fairies get their power from?"

The girl didn't have to think. She knew the answer instantly, "From their imagination."

"That's right. I'm picking up impressions from you. I'm not alone in having a special place. Am I?"

The girl shook her head sadly. "It's that place I told you about in my story."

"A place so like mine. It inspires me!"

"But last time I saw it, it was burning and there were flames! And then the wind finished it off."

The girl was looking too unhappy for the old man to bear.

"You saw your special place at its finest. Now it seems lost to you. But let me give you some encouragement, Avery Smith."

The old man smiled kindly. The girl waited for him to speak. But she heard only silence. The silence enveloped her like his aura of gentleness all around her.

The gentlest fingers closed her eyelids. The Wizard had summoned Mother Sleep. Together they broke the silence with a lullaby. And their song sounded to Avery like birds welcoming the dawn.

But the most welcome sound to her was the distant notes of a piccolo being played.

The notes flew with the birds. The birds flew with the notes.

The End

THE CASE STUDY OF CHILD A

Maeve Underhill was a psychologist and psychical researcher. She worked with children in the 1970s and made her name after discovering Child A, an eleven-year-old girl with possible psychic ability. Originally published in the *Journal of Psychical Research,* Maeve's case study includes a recollection of when the two met.

Maeve writes *I knew within minutes of meeting Child A that she was just the kind of girl that I had been looking for. She was friendly and willing to talk about her experiences. Once she had a language in which to talk about them.*

That she experienced nature in a divine light didn't make her exceptional. Hundreds of thousands of people have mystical experiences. In some, the experience has a long lasting effect on their life. In Child A the experience was of such intensity that she never shook off the feeling of wonder.

My work with children has shown me that a divine light shines brighter in children, because they are innocent. Adults are too disillusioned and their shuttered minds are blind to the glories all around them.

I felt humbled talking to this child mystic. The way she would speak about the Garden made you want to believe in it. Real or not the Garden is "a good place to be."

Child A appears very advanced for her age. She's very literate and self-aware but that doesn't stop her having a child's mindset. To an adult the Garden makes sense as a mythical Eden, one we long to return to - a place of harmony and peace. We know dream symbols are archetypes: universal ideas and images inherited from our ancestors.

Child A doesn't much care for archetypes. Myths and fairy tales are more to her taste. And it is through the lens of magic and folklore that she finds truth in her dreams.

What is of interest to psychology and psychical research is her power over the imagination. For those in her presence, the mythical can become convincingly real.

There is more to her than this though. Visions are meant to be private. But in her case this isn't so.

Those in sympathy with her can see, hear and feel; whatever she believes she can see, hear and feel.

I haven't got round to investigating her friends yet. They too interest me. I suspect they also share her gift. They alike have the power to travel to and from Dream Worlds.

(Maeve concludes with a mystery) *The parents of Child A have just this moment telephoned me to inform me their daughter has disappeared!*

Now, whilst vanishing isn't unusual for Child A, this current disappearance is so much more mystifying than usual. She was upstairs in her bedroom and outside it was pouring with rain!

I suspect she's gone looking for that garden of hers.

I wish she wouldn't worry about its fate. What she perceives as the Garden is all the light and life that she carries within her.

FLOWERS AND FAES

Dream of a garden from infant days
When your playmates were flowers and Faes
When love for you shone out from the friendliest gaze
When acceptance seemed genuine and not just a phase
If you know the Garden under any of its names
Its peace will be present in you and fuel further games
Rejection is unknown here, there's only joy in the gaze
That's enshrined in your memory with the flowers and Faes
Their love is a lifeline in dark insane days
So join hands with them and bless their infant ways

Join hands with them and bless infant ways

GIRL WITH IMAGINATION OF WIZARDS

The Girl with the Imagination of Wizards
is a wiz with a deck of Cards
She won't pretend they can tell your fortune
But what she does with them is just as hard

She'll convince you that the world doesn't have to lose its wonder
Not when she can blast your ears by clapping louder than thunder!

You'll be happy to lose to this girl
and gain a vision of life
Because she's a victor with a winning tale
Her spirit is blithe

The Girl with the Imagination of Wizard
is Queen of all bards
She holds happiness in her hands
in a pack of unbeatable cards

GLOSSARY

ARCHETYPES:

Jungian archetypes are a concept from psychology that refers to a universal, inherited idea, or image, that is present in the collective unconscious of all human beings. Archetypes are thought to be the basis of many of the common themes and symbols that appear in stories, myths, and dreams across different cultures and societies. The concept of the collective unconscious was first proposed by Carl Jung, a Swiss psychiatrist and psychoanalyst.

Jung differentiated between two types of dreams: Big Dreams and Little Dreams. Big Dreams revolve around powerful archetypal images from the collective unconscious. They carry profound meaning and play an important role in the process of self-discovery and realizing our true self.

Little Dreams are more mundane and may reflect everyday experiences or random brain activity.

BRAZEN HEADS:

A brazen head, brass head, or bronze head was a legendary automaton in the early modern period whose ownership was ascribed to late medieval scholars, such as Roger Bacon, who had developed a reputation as Wizards. Made of brass or bronze, the male head was variously mechanical or magical.

CHANGELING:

A child believed to have been secretly substituted by fairies for the parents' real child in infancy.

FAIRY, FAIRIES OR FAERIE

A fairy is a mythical, legendary creature found in the folklore of multiple European cultures, where it is a kind of spirit with supernatural powers. Myths and tales about fairies do not have a single origin, but are rather a collection of "folk beliefs" from different sources.

Various folk theories about the origins of fairies portray them as either demoted angels or demons (as in Christian tradition). Or as deities in pagan belief systems. Other explanations are that they are the spirits of the deceased.

Fairies have also been theorised to be the prehistoric precursors to humans, or have been accepted as nature spirits.

"Fairy" has been used as an adjective with a meaning equivalent to "enchanted" or "magical." It is also used as a name for the places these beings come from: the Land of Fairy, or Faerie.

Fairies, Faes and Changelings may appear to be a quant superstition today but they were feared by our ancestors. Changelings were believed to be inhuman imposters and the belief served as a justification for infanticide.

HEELSTONE:

The Heel Stone is a single large block of sarsen stone standing within the Avenue outside the entrance of the Stonehenge earthwork in Wiltshire. Traditionally, the Heel Stone marks the place on the horizon where the summer solstice sunrise appears when viewed from the centre of the stone circle. Every year thousands of people gather to watch this event

SEELIE COURT:

The Seelie Court is a group of fairies, often specified as good fairies who contrast with the wicked Unseelie Court. The Seelie Court were those fairies who seek help from humans, warn those who have accidentally offended them, and return human kindness with favours of their own. Still a fairy belonging to this court could avenge insults and could be prone to mischief. Conversely, the Unseelie Court were the darkly-inclined fairies who would attack without provocation.

THE LEGEND OF THE CHANGELING

This folklore friendly fragment commonly believed to be the work of a young female bard is one of the first stories told about Bobby. Like most of the lore on Bobby, it began as an aural work and it was only after becoming a written work that it began to be more widely circulated.

As scholars have noted the lore on Bobby is full of contradictions and exaggerations, often borrowing from older tales and in the process updating them and giving them a more contemporary meaning. This early legend is consistent with the majority of other tales told about Bobby: - 'The Boy from the Age of Wizards'.

There once was a village in the county of Gloucestershire, near the Forest of Dean, whose inhabitants still followed the old religion but in a misguided and bloodthirsty way. They were a village of tree fellers and miners and life for them was hard - so hard, they couldn't support 'weaklings' or 'suffer them to live'. This most charitable of people had developed a primitive religion, one that allowed them to get rid of the least productive members of society under the guise of pagan piety.

Those unlucky enough to be born with defects rendering them unable to meet the standard of perfection demanded by the village were consigned to the flames! The Mayday festivities were particularly bloody and the bonfires that were lit then were not for amusement only.

Pity the child who was not normal, could not pass as normal, at least his life was short. Such a child could not hope to appeal to parents, nor to family, as his or her kin were often the most active participants in the Sabbath rites.

After all, a changeling wasn't a real child. No! They were merely a 'fairy substitute'.

This is the story of one such child. A boy named Bobby. This boy was not weak or unproductive but instead was much too wise for his parent's liking.

The story begins with a woman called Willow who was married to a handsome, well-built man called Ash; who had risen from humble beginnings and was about to become the chief warlock of this damnable village.

An often inebriated, quick tempered, man. He had all the virtues needed to take on the role of sacred executioner!

The couple had been married for seven years but despite their good health and 'normality', they remained childless.

Willow cursed her empty womb and sobbed nightly for a child while Ash grew ever more angry and prone to violent outbursts. Woe to anyone who dared question his fertility.

The Chief Warlock didn't have to know any *real magic* (his role was purely ceremonial) but one thing he mustn't be was infertile. Fearing for their safety and for Ash's position in the village, if they continued without child, the couple turned their minds to the Good People.

"Our village is at war with the Good People," Ash glowered, "They steal our children and leave monsters behind. Let us not waste any more time in lovemaking, but let us see how the Gentry like it when it's their turn to lose a child."

This was too much for Willow. "Please, husband, I don't want trouble with the Gentry; let us not offend them. Besides, I don't want a fairy brat. Just a human child. Let us ask nicely for such a child."

And so it was agreed that Willow would venture into the nearby forest under cover of night and seek the Good People's aid. Husband and wife knew no closeness after this time, and Ash didn't even look upon his wife's nakedness as she left his side, to make her way along the forest path.

The twilight air rang with the high, clear voices of the forest fairies - all joined together in elvish song. Imagine Willow's naked feet pressing down upon the bluebells carpeting the forest floor, and the new moon shining upon her earthly prettiness as she enters a small clearing surrounded by trees.

What Willow saw next astonished her and it is no wonder that the Good People took offence.

Not for mortal eyes the whirl of lights inside the creeping curls of mist setting the atmosphere aquiver. If she had left after the dance she might have escaped unscathed - but foolishly she stayed on to see more. Willow saw the great and the good of Fairyland and shuddered with pleasure and fear. She could make out fairies, hags and patriarchs and crept closer to the company to see what they were looking at.

The scene before her was incredible enough to make a painting or even a poem. Willow envied the talents of the painter or poet that could capture scenes from Fairyland and give them immortality. Willow was not a painter or a poet, so 'Now' was all she had. And 'Now' she was looking out from behind bars.

With a shock, she realized what those bars were.

How tall the grass is grown. How small I am. Tis fairy magic! So it's true. Fairies can make anything – even their own bodies - any size they want it to be.

Her awe at the unnaturally high grass ended once she noticed its resemblance to a forest.

Ash's axe could cut through those stems and make short work of the fairy trees. Do Fairies have axes? And what would they use them for if they did?

She did not have long to wait for an answer for an aged voice broke the silence with a command.

"Crack it open! Quick, now! Crack the great hazelnut open!"

Willow was almost in the centre of the clearing now, impatient to see what was happening and not quite believing what she saw.

Do my eyes deceive me? Is there really a fairy woodsman and is he really holding an axe? And how do I know that Queen Mab has arranged the whole thing just so she can have a new carriage? Oh, but I see the Queen, and her mind is open to me. That Feller better crack that nut open quick, or she'll ensure his head cracks open instead.

The fairy woodsman was concentrating, his axe held aloft; ready to bring it down upon the hazelnut as the old man had bidden.

"Crack it, open!" cried the aged voice.

Willow could now see the speaker. A white-bearded old man was standing behind the Feller. "Do it singly. Make single double. Or there'll be trouble, tonight."

Willow held her breath. All motion had somehow become frozen in an unmoving tableau. She wanted to warn the Feller for his axe remained poised: suspended in the-air.

She did not know what she did to give herself away but suddenly the tableau unfroze again. This was her chance to ask for a child.

Now, the Gentry may have looked small amongst all that verdure but Willow still found them awe-inspiring, and mindful of her mission she had just began to introduce herself when the whole lot of them disappeared.

Their departure was noisy and it frightened her. They made angry buzzing sounds, which made her ears ring terribly, and if she hadn't closed her eyes when she did, she would have been blinded by the weird glowing light emanating from their bodies.

Next thing she knew it was morning and she was lying face down upon the grass. Her body was smarting and her flesh showed the marks where the Gentry had tried wounding her with their arrows. What was worse a horrid cobweb-like material covered her face. She clawed at it desperately, finding it difficult to get off her.

Willow so hated the Fair Folk, for this, that she vowed never to ask for their help again; and to spite them she snatched up the hazelnut lying abandoned on the grass.

No carriage for the Queen Bee! She doesn't deserve a lovely hazelnut carriage to ride in. As for painting and poetry, or capturing Fairy Land, that's nonsense! Weak dangerous nonsense! The kind of thing I've been brought up to despise.

Her husband was drunk when she returned, thankfully postponing any admission of failure from her. But once the drink had worn off, and Willow confessed to disaster, he seemed strangely elated.

"You've done well, wife. We shall keep their precious tree fruit. Let's see what comes of it when they come to get it back!"

Knowing that fairies feared iron, the couple found an old iron strongbox to put the hazelnut in. They locked the box then hid the key.

When Mab realised the nut was missing, she sent for the oldest maid in the palace and took her in her confidence.

"We left in such a hurry that we forgot the very thing that made our meeting necessary. Return and bring the nut back to me at once! Please, be extra careful though. We cannot protect you as well as you'd wish. Remember, you once married a mortal man. You rebelled against duty. So think of this as *making amends*."

And so to a drab home, that held little charm, came one of the oldest of the Gentry. How easy it was to trap her in a fishing net (that had seen better days). How terrified the maid - how powerless to resist, when her glinting, fluttering, silvery silhouette of a body was transferred from the fishing net to the iron strongbox containing the nut.

Emboldened by her tears of despair the couple made their request, they asked for a little boy; a hard-working little boy who would do all the heavy work for them and prove to the villagers that the husband wasn't infertile.

Their captive had no choice but to give in, and so by way of a message, she conveyed the couple's demands via a song sent into the ether on wings of sorrow.

Little did the couple know the consternation their theft had caused, and how not one but two Queens were involved in the response.

Mab was virtually the sole ruler of Faerie now, but her predecessor, Titania, held on to her own unique powers and still had a little authority. As it was, Titania alone possessed the unique relationship with Time that would allow her to choose the changeling boy.

Titania's criteria for choosing would be more moral than Mab's; she would choose a boy strong enough to survive ill treatment, one with qualities that could win over uncaring hearts (and humanise them). She chose a Wizard's son that would fit into any environment.

One joyous day, in spring, Willow became a mother. The village Doctor attended the couple in private, and once the "baby boy" was old enough to be seen in public, every single doubter in the village were forced to admit they'd been wrong about the husband's fertility.

The couple named the boy Robert, but for a nickname they called him Robin; their hope was that young Robert, or Robin, or Bobby, would grow up to be a devil of a man! just like his father.

Alas, poor Bobby wasn't loved or celebrated for long. His infancy was not so bad but his teenage years started horribly.

He turned out to be too strange for the couple's tastes, and unwilling to admit his true parentage they decided to keep their secret at all costs. *But the teenager must be made to suffer for their disappointment and he'd never be given a chance to grow idle.*

"He must work, and work, harder than any horse or beast; it is only right as we are kind enough to let him live on."

But alas, working isn't easy when the flesh on your bones starts to sag. And how much work can you do when your spirit is near breaking? Poor Bobby started wasting away, so much so, that the couple started thinking the flames would make a nice end for him, after all.

The little captive in her iron cell was no less fortunate. She too was pining and wasting away. Her light was dull now. But her ceaseless cries of pain and betrayal were not in vain. They alerted the boy to her presence and saved the pair of them from unending misery.

Now Bobby, whatever other talents he possessed, had exceptionally keen hearing. He could hear her tiny, muffled cries, and he pitied her on hearing her distress. He knew better than to ask his parents who the mystery woman was that cried so mournfully when he was left on his own. He just knew the cries were real and that there was someone else in the house with him.

Bobby puzzled over the meaning behind the cries and he was no less baffled by his dreams. For the mysterious woman didn't just cry, she sang too! and the time she chose for singing was when the family were in bed.

Ash and Willow slept through her songs but Bobby was more receptive to them, and so they made their way into his dreams (changing them for the better). He would often wake up in the morning, with a tune in his head, having emerged from sleep with visions of a barely remembered paradise:

Dream of a garden from infant days
When your playmates were flowers and Faes
When love for you shone out from the friendliest gaze
When acceptance seemed genuine and not just a phase

If you know the Garden under any of its names

Its peace will be present in you and fuel further games
You'll recall your playmates: the flowers and Faes
Now join hands with them and bless their infant ways

Poetry was not nonsense to Bobby. It cheered him to wake up with her words on his lips: words that warmed his heart and gave him consolation for a loss he was barely aware of.

It was approaching May Day, or Beltane, an important date in the pagan calendar, and it was well for the teenager's peace of mind that he didn't spend much time out of doors and so he remained blissfully ignorant of the village and its macabre goings on.

He didn't' see any harm in the corn dollies in the cottage kitchens, or find anything to fret about in the Maypole erected on the village green, or even suspect there was a wicker statue due to be be aired on the 1st of May. His parents' absences were put down to socializing, or merry making, a way of celebrating the coming of the harvest.

Those very absences were an opportunity for Bobby to search the house.

"This poor creature, well, she sounds like a she, must be a prisoner like myself. I am no loved child. I'm also in jail!"

So Bobby searched the upper stories of the house; he searched the lower stories too, he even searched the garden, the shed; even the rickety outdoor privy was inspected but all to no avail.

He searched when his parents were asleep, or when they were too busy fighting each other to keep an eye out on their 'miscreant child'.

Beltane came at last! Celebrations began. Cattle were put out to pasture, and everyone looked forward to the crowning of the May Queen, and the lighting of bonfires!

Bobby still did not suspect the role his parents' had prepared for him. Even workhorses need feeding and can outlive their usefulness! Besides Beltane was a time to make sacrifices. The couple had decided to offer up their child.

Ash laughed at the boy's ignorance.

He was rarely sober now but when he was how eagerly he anticipated the handing over of power from the old Warlock to his younger successor.

The old Warlock had grown too weak to command respect, anymore; he would join the children in the wicker statues! Ash never doubted his right to take the old man's place.

Willow was hardly better. Although she sometimes regretted what they had done, she had become so hardened to life her chest might as well have contained an empty husk with no fruit inside. But even Willow found her husband's jibes in bad taste.

"Give him extra work," Ash thumped the beer-soaked tabletop at the village tavern. "Make him work real hard. So once he's done, he can go into the flames with our blessing."

Ash said this just before passing out; therefore missing the onset of tears in his wife's eyes. He was not the only villager to succumb to the drink, that day. And the tavern, in which the cruel celebrants had come together to toast the sacrifices, soon rang with the sound of a village snoring.

Willow couldn't wait to join the menfolk, she didn't want to stay awake and be alone with her thoughts. Soon she too was asleep. But her dreams were uneasy, as they all revolved around an angry Mab.

You did not release your captive, as promised. You've kept what you stole.

Ash dreamed of the fair Titania. No less angry was she, although regretful and contrite.

I took the boy from the care of a loving father. Oh, absent-minded wizard! He knew not what he signed. His boy, his poor boy! His stay away from the Garden has grown overlong. It's becoming an exile!

Mab took revenge on the sleeping village.

They would not wake up to bonfires or child captives. They would not wake up at all.

Bobby continued working while all this was going on. But he made sure to finish his most urgent chores, first, so that he would have time to solve the mystery that haunted the household.

Once free to search he spent hours looking all over the house: covering every inch of its grounds. There wasn't a ladder he wouldn't climb, a corner he wouldn't peer into, or a piece of furniture he wouldn't look behind.

He was running out of places to inspect when he decided to

look inside his father's shed again

The shed was his father's domain. It contained all Ash's fishing gear and gardening tools. His father had never taken him fishing. It never occurred to Ash to take Bobby with him. Catching fish was not for the likes of Bobby not when he could be left behind to do the gardening.

The little iron strongbox was so clearly visible sat upon the shelf, just beneath the dark stained beam of oak, that it was a wonder Bobby hadn't noticed it earlier.

"Help! Bobby! Help!"

"I will. I will. Oh, where are you? You sound like you're near."

"I'm here! Quick, Bobby. Smash open the iron box. Set me free. Do it now! Please!"

Bobby struggled with the strongbox. It wouldn't open. How could it? There was no key. With no more time to waste, he picked up the box and threw it against the wall. Smack! A little door flew open in it; just as the box began descending towards the floor.

Bobby blinked. There was a flash of light and something "fairylike," started flickering in the corner of his eye.

Then lips kissed his forehead. A voice told him "to have no fear;" before whispering his name, then leaving him in perplexity.

The presence returned almost instantly it had gone. There were things it needed to tell him.

First, it gave a warning. He was in danger and must leave his parent's home. Join with others and help them escape. Start a new life in the forest, or beyond.

Then there came a promise. One day he would find a new home; he would have friends; a woman that he could love and they would know peace.

Village life resumed without Bobby and the children.

The burials were many, that season, but none of the deaths were expected. Instead of children, many adults died!

The heartless couple never woke up from their sleep. They had disappointed the expectations of Titania, and enraged Mab.

As for Bobby he would have many happier adventures in the

future, but not until his mind had blotted out most of his past. He did, one day, find love. But that is another story.

Printed in Great Britain
by Amazon

44976162R00056